LOPEZ

AN EIDOLON BLACK OPS NOVEL: BOOK 9

MADDIE WADE

Lopez
An Eidolon Black Ops Novel: Book 9
By Maddie Wade

Published by Maddie Wade

Cover: Envy Creative Designs
Editing: Black Opal Editing
Formatting: Black Opal Editing

COPYRIGHT

ACKNOWLEDGMENTS

I am so lucky to have such an amazing team around me without which I could never bring my books to life. I am so grateful to have you in my life, you are more than friends you are so essential to my life.

My wonderful beta team, Greta and Deanna who are brutally honest and beautifully kind. If it is rubbish you tell me it is, and if you love it you are effusive. Your support means so much to me.

My editor—Linda at Black Opal Editing, who is so patient, she is so much more than an editor she is a teacher and friend.

Thank you to my group Maddie's Minxes, your support and love for Fortis, Eidolon, Ryoshi, and all the books I write is so important to me. Special thanks to Rowena, Tracey, Faith, Rachel, Carolyn, Kellie, Maria, Greta, Deanna, Sharon, and Linda L for making the group such a friendly place to be.

My Arc Team for not keeping me on edge too long while I wait for feedback.

Lastly and most importantly thank you to my readers who have embraced my books so wholeheartedly and shown a love for the stories in my head. To hear you say that you see my characters as family makes me so humble and proud. I hope you enjoy Lopez and Addie as much as I did.

DEDICATION

For Lily

PROLOGUE

ADELINE WALKED on shaky legs back to her room in the Ravelino mansion. The muggy air of the Mexican summer clung to her skin and made her crave the cool shower awaiting her. More than that, she needed to scrub the feel of Juan Ravelino's touch from her skin.

She'd known an undercover case like this would steal parts of her, but she was best placed to find the intel they needed to stop Juan from moving forward with his nuclear arms deals.

She stepped into her room and locked the door, knowing it gave her no more safety from the armed guards that stood outside her room than if she'd left it unlocked. The façade of safety was something she desperately needed tonight though. Stripping the red piece of silk from her body that Juan had picked out for her to wear, she stepped under the cold water and grabbed the soap, trying to scrub the feel of his hands away.

Tears coursed down her cheeks, the only warmth on her skin were the bits that were red from the cloth she'd used to erase the sick, twisted man's touch. She hadn't been a virgin when she'd arrived but now she felt brutalised in a way she'd never imagined. Yes, she was CIA, but this was taking it too far.

Bruises on her wrists and ankles attested to the night's hideous games and she'd had to pretend at every turn that she was there because she loved Juan. That she craved his touch when the truth was, she hated him. He showered her with gifts and treated her like a doll to be played with. She still didn't have the information she needed to stop him but she had to get out.

Switching off the shower she fought a shiver and wrapped a towel around her body. She needed to get a message to her handler and have him extract her. Her hand lowered to her belly where her child, conceived with a man she didn't trust, nestled. She didn't know how it had happened. She'd been given the shot because of this very risk and yet she couldn't deny she was pregnant, and it was getting too dangerous for her to stay in this luxury prison dressed up as a beautiful mansion.

At first, she'd thought to terminate her pregnancy but seeing those two pink lines she'd known that this baby was innocent, that she or he had no part in this and she'd do whatever it took to get her child to safety, and away from the Ravelino cartel.

Feeling more energised now she didn't have the sickly stink of Juan's aftershave in her nose, or his touch lingering on her skin, she dressed in black yoga pants and a dark grey singlet. She tied her running shoes, her still flat belly giving no hint at this early stage to her condition and stood. That wouldn't last long she knew. At five feet four inches she was hardly big and any day now her pregnancy would start to show as her body was already changing.

The guards were used to her running around the compound and merely leered when she walked out of the room and past them. Juan liked her slim figure and had given her free rein to run where he allowed it. She'd prefer more privacy to make this call, but beggars couldn't be choosers.

"When the boss finishes with you, you want some of this cock?"

Osvaldo, the guard she hated the most, grabbed her by her upper arm and pushed his pelvis against her hip, his erection evident. Adeline fought the shiver and instead gave him a cold look. "Never and he hasn't finished with me yet. So unless you want me to tell him how you touched what was his, take your fucking hands off me." She didn't have to inject any coldness into her words because she felt it.

Osvaldo shoved her away and she stumbled, making him smile. "Puta."

Adeline didn't look back as she heard him and the other guard laughing but ran out of the mansion and let the fragrant night air soothe her battered soul. She resisted the urge to run her hand over her belly as she jogged the perimeter of the compound. She knew cameras watched her every move and a guard was placed in every blind spot except one.

There was a small rose garden towards the back of the property where the guards never went because behind it was the area where the guard dogs slept. Nobody would get past them, so they didn't bother with cameras or checking. Adeline moved into the area, holding her hand out for the dogs to sniff before feeding them the cheese she'd brought out there earlier. Knowing she didn't have much time she gave one more furtive look around before hitting dial.

Her handler Joel Hansen picked up. She gave the code to prove it was her and waited.

"Go."

"I need an urgent extract. My safety has been compromised."

"How?"

Adeline hated how cold and clinical he was. He'd been warm and charming when she'd met him. Just like a fool she'd trusted him and given him her body. A decision she couldn't regret now because it had given her the child she carried. She hadn't seen it at first, but Joel was a climber of the worst kind and she no longer felt safe with him watching her back. He'd made it very clear their one night had been just that and meant nothing. She should tell him about the baby, that it was his, but something held her back.

"Juan is making these encounters far too violent."

Hansen knew exactly what she was talking about, he had been the one who insisted it was necessary that she sleep with the man and refused to extract her, forcing her hand and making her hate the fact she'd ever let him touch her.

"Define."

"I'm covered in bruises."

"Are they life threatening?"

Adeline couldn't believe what she was hearing. "Not yet but it's only a matter of time."

"We can't afford for you to blow this op. We need actionable intelligence."

Adeline knew she wouldn't get any help from him. He was hanging her out to dry. "Fine." She hung up and looked at her phone. She had a decision to make now, one that would have far-reaching consequences but as she thought of the child she carried, she knew she didn't have a choice.

She dialled a number she knew by heart. It was picked up immediately and she felt relief flow through her.

"Three am tomorrow. Exactly where you're standing. Be ready."

The call dropped out and Adeline felt the first rush of relief in her blood. Her team, her friends, were coming for her. The Navy SEAL team who'd run her first op when she was a case officer had stayed in touch and Brand Navarro, the Master Chief, had always told her if she needed him and his team to call that number and she'd be extracted.

Adeline had no idea how they knew where she was but the fact they did made her feel less alone for the first time since she'd left her position with the team. She'd never dreamed of doing this work, it had never been her goal. Science was her passion and somewhere along the line she'd gotten off track.

Adeline stashed her phone in her bra and ran back out of the cover, doing a loop of the compound so the guards could catch her on camera before going back to her room. She passed Osvaldo who ignored her but heard him laugh as she closed her door.

"Stupid puta has no idea that bitches don't leave here unless it's in a body bag."

She'd heard the rumours of Juan's cruel sexual appetites, and now, having had them forced on her she believed them. Her hand on her belly, she spoke softly so only her baby could hear her. "One more night and we'll be safe."

She prayed to any deity who'd listen it was true, and she could make it through the next twenty-four hours unscathed. She was sick of living with a pit of fear squirming in her belly from worry she'd be caught or exposed at any second. She wanted out of this life, she wanted peace. The price was simply too high to pay for a country that treated her like she didn't matter. Sleep was fitful that night, flashes of vivid dreams where she was covered in blood and running for her life haunted her when she woke. Every time she rounded the corner expecting to find the exit, she found only dead ends. She awoke tired and edgy, her nerves frayed, and her nausea back with a vengeance.

She went about her day, relieved that Juan was away from the mansion on business. He never told her his plans, but she'd make one more attempt to find the files she needed. She needed to access the computer in his study which he kept locked; the key hung around his neck on a chain. He was a paranoid bastard, which was why he never seemed to get caught.

Slipping from her room she went and got breakfast, smiling at Eva, the cook who was kneading bread. She helped herself to orange juice and toast hoping it would stay down. She needed the energy after her sleepless night and the plans for later. She thanked her lucky stars when the food stayed down and waved to Eva as she left the kitchen. The people there would never help her, and she'd be a fool to trust them but that didn't mean some weren't nice to her, and Eva the cook and Mia the housekeeper had always been friendly.

She waited an hour to make sure Iago wouldn't arrive as he sometimes did when his brother was away and left her room, her lock pick in her pocket. If they caught her, they'd kill her but not before torturing her. Adeline walked the long hallway on the ground floor, the polished wood clicking under her heels as she moved with confidence. Half of her job was to act like she had the right to be in places she shouldn't be.

She glanced at the cameras inside the house. Because Juan had business meetings he didn't want others to know about, this section of the house wasn't covered. It made her job so much easier. She reached the double doors of the study and quickly looked behind her before she took a breath and went to work on the lock. She'd done this so many times it was second nature. Practice always made perfect, and study was one of her favourite things. She was a student at heart and should have stayed in the sciences where learning was almost a moment-by-moment process. Instead, she'd been seduced by the excitement and glamour of this life. Something she now whole-heartedly regretted.

The click told her she was in, and she carefully lowered the handle and slipped inside, closing the door softly. The room reeked of cigar smoke and aftershave, and it made her belly churn. Fighting back a wave of nausea, she moved to the computer. Turning it on, she cursed seeing it was password protected. She tried a few and failed before she rolled her lip between her teeth and considered Juan. Her eyes moved around the room looking for inspiration. It was all wood panelling and leather, with priceless art on the walls, which frankly, she found hideous.

One thing Juan had was a terrible memory for the mundane and a password would fall into that category for him. Her eyes caught on a picture hanging on the wall opposite the desk called Waterlily and she shrugged knowing it was as good a plan as any other. Adeline gasped and smiled to herself when it worked. Slipping a thumb drive from her pocket she plugged it in and began to download the data. She didn't know what, if anything, she'd get but this was her last hurrah.

The sound of vehicles moving up the drive had her heart hammering in her throat as she raced to the window. Iago's Porsche was pulling through the gate, which meant she had two minutes before he entered the house and caught her.

Adeline could feel her heart beating in her chest like it wanted to hammer out of her body and hated it. She'd never thrived on adrenaline like others did. She watched the download reach ninety percent and heard the Porsche get closer, almost to the house. As the download finished, she yanked it from the drive, used her shaky hands to power the computer down, and slipped from the room, relocking the door, and dashing back to her room.

She was closing her bedroom door as the front door opened and Iago strolled inside. A few minutes later she heard him go into Juan's study and wondered what he was up to. Juan never allowed anyone in there without him, not even his brother. She paced her room knowing it would be a long day of waiting and decided to try and nap.

That evening she went through the same routine of changing into her running gear but this time she'd have to get out unseen knowing the guards wouldn't permit her to go for a run in the middle of the night.

Dragging a pale blue silk house gown over her clothes, she opened the door. Thankfully, Osvaldo was off as she had no desire to run into that asshole. She gave a short nod at the two men guarding her room and walked to the kitchen. She'd got up during the night to get food several times before, trying to establish random patterns that would work and make her seem invisible as she moved around the compound that imprisoned her. Juan hadn't come back but some of his guards had, which wasn't unusual. He often sent them to the house when he was with other women.

As she entered the kitchen, she was relieved to find it empty. She began making noise, pouring milk into a pan and putting it on the stove to boil. The guard in the hall should hear her and think nothing of it for a while, at least long enough for her to slip out through the servant's entrance. She knew it was often unlocked as the kitchen staff would pop out for a smoke.

The night was warm, and she could feel the sweat on the back of her neck under her long, thick hair. She'd rather have it up out of her way, but she'd needed to look like she'd been in bed. Scurrying along the edge of the property, she halted at the corner and waited for the guard to turn, the ember of his cigarette amplified by the darkness.

The one thing in her favour was the fact that Ravelino's guards had gotten sloppy. They were so used to the fear Juan and his brother Iago evoked that nobody had dared attack them for years. That now worked in her favour and she was happy his men were lazy. Adeline knew after tonight a few would die and he'd amp up his security, making it that much harder for the next CIA operator to infiltrate his compound.

Adeline felt a stab of guilt for abandoning her post and fleeing with the threat very much still in play, but she had to think about her child. At least she had the drive, and once she'd seen what was on it she'd decide what to do with it all. With that in mind, she darted across the lawn and headed for the roses. It was two minutes until her extraction time, and she knew Brand and his men were like clockwork.

She took a moment to let the dogs sniff her, the last thing she needed was them alerting the guards. Her head throbbed with the start of a headache from the tension, her plan for a nap thwarted when Iago had asked her to have lunch with him. She couldn't refuse without making him suspicious so she'd eaten the beautifully prepared meal and drunk the minimal amount of wine she could get away with. Refusing would be an insult and Iago was a proud man, perhaps even worse than his brother, and would take offence at the slight.

He'd questioned her on Juan's movements, and she'd been vague, which was easy as he never shared his plans with her. She knew he was up to something and wondered if he was about to betray his older brother.

A sound behind her made her turn quickly, her hands up in self-defence. A face she recognised came into view, covered in camouflage and smiling.

"Brand!" She moved to him, wrapping her arms around her friend, feeling safe as he enfolded her in his arms.

"Come on, bug, time to go."

Adeline loved the nickname he'd given her after talking about the nicknames she and her beloved sister Astrid used. He'd said bumble-bees were bugs and it had stuck.

"Hustle has the car one click away. Can you run it?" He was steering her toward a rope ladder hung over the wall and concealed by the trees.

"Yes."

Brand was carrying an automatic weapon and urged her to move as he covered her six, just like the old days. She was halfway up when she heard a shout followed by a gunshot.

"Shit. Time to move, bug."

Adeline moved quicker, throwing her leg over the wall as a hand grabbed for her and Santa appeared, named because of his shock of white hair and beard, but certainly not because of his belly. The man was hot, like a grey-haired, sexy, biker Santa and the best explosives expert she knew.

"Hey, Addie, give me your hand."

He hauled her over the wall, the brick scrapping the skin from her palms, but she didn't feel any pain, just the taste of freedom. She jumped to the ground as Santa put down cover fire for Brand.

She kept moving toward Hustle who was in the jeep and climbed inside, her eyes on the outside of the mansion walls as she waited for her friends. Her breath left her in relief when Brand and Santa ran towards the vehicle and jumped in, Brand beside her and Santa in the passenger's seat.

Hustle floored it, driving like a pro, hence his name. They heard shots fired behind them, but the sound faded as they got further away.

"Well, aren't you a sight for sore eyes." Brand lifted his arm and she leaned into it.

He was the brother she'd never had. They all were, and she loved them. "I missed you guys."

"Missed you too, sweetheart. Wanna tell us what's going on so I can make a plan for you?"

Adeline explained the situation with her handler and her pregnancy, watching the looks on the men's faces growing darker and darker. Joel had never been popular with the Teams and even less so now.

They stopped in a field in the middle of nowhere and climbed onto a chopper. She found herself sandwiched between Hustle and Santa as Brand sat opposite. The earphones on her head startled her when Brand spoke.

"Bug, you know you need to disappear, right?"

Adeline sighed, she'd known that the CIA would never let her live and even if they did, Juan Ravelino wouldn't. Not after she'd humiliated him by escaping. "I know."

"I have a friend in Alaska who can set you up with a new life, new name, identity, the lot but you won't ever be able to contact the people you love again. Not your sister or your parents."

Her hand went to her belly and Brand tracked it, his eyes going soft as he reached for her hand. "I know it's tough, bug, but you have to die to protect your baby. It's the only way."

"What about you guys? Can I stay in touch with you?"

"Not at first, but maybe after a few years we can come for a visit."

"It's cold in Alaska."

"It *is* fucking cold, but it's vast, like the waste land of the world and it will keep you safe."

Adeline gave a short nod. "Thank you for always having my back."

"Of course, you're family."

"Brand, can I ask one last favour?"

"Of course."

"Will you look out for Astrid for me? Just from a distance to make sure she stays safe."

"As much as is possible, yes."

With that, her fate was set and a new life away from everyone she loved was put in motion.

Six months later, as her daughter lay on her chest looking up at her sleepily after a sixteen-hour labour, she knew it had been worth it.

CHAPTER ONE

HE SAT BY HER BED, his laptop open, working to find the answers he needed to solve this mystery. Adeline Lasson was part of his past nobody knew about. Not even Jack or Will knew of the connection they shared, but he did. From the second he'd heard her name fall from Astrid's lips the pieces had come together, falling into place.

Yet, before he could get the answers he so desperately needed, she was beaten, her voice silenced, and the answers he sought stolen once again. Lopez pushed his hair from his face, exhaustion once again plaguing him, but sleep was a rare thing for him. His mind was unable to relax and let go of the questions until his body took the choice from him and he collapsed into a deep sleep for twelve to fifteen hours, often waking feeling groggy and confused.

Jack understood his limits and knew of his past. He'd made no secret of who he was and what his past was or his desire to escape it, but nobody knew about the tether that kept him by the bed of the one woman he hoped held the answers.

He should tell Jack the truth, tell Astrid, but after everything they'd been through, he had no desire to be the one to add more complications to their lives. There'd be time for that when Adeline woke—if she woke.

He'd been by her bedside for months. So much so, he knew her condition better than anyone, and there was no reason for her coma, at least not a physical one. Her body had healed, and her brain showed no irregularities from her injury, but that was where the complexities of the human body and mind came into play. The injuries she'd suffered were predictably unpredictable.

They'd never met or spoken in person, and yet he felt like he knew her, and he'd had the overwhelming desire to protect her and keep her safe from the people who hunted her. Looking back at his computer, he knew it would be quicker to go to Will and ask him to find the information he needed, but he also knew once that pandora's box was opened, it couldn't be put back, and Adeline would be in danger once more.

Her finger twitched, and he placed the computer beside him and took her fingers in his. He noticed she got agitated easily and if he held her hand and spoke to her, she eased. "It's okay, Addie. Nobody is going to hurt you. You're safe, and I won't let anyone harm you ever again."

Instead of easing, her heart rate became more erratic, and she began to thrash around the bed until he had to stand, afraid she'd hurt herself. He hit the bell for the nurse who came running in to see what was wrong.

"I'll find the doctor."

Not knowing what else to do, Lopez sat on the bed and wrapped her lightly in his arms to stop her from hitting herself against the bars on the bed. As he looked down at her a sob escaped her, cracking his heart in two at the pain inside it. Her eyes flew open, and he saw the bright green orbs for the first time. Fear clouded her face as she grasped at his arms, desperately weak but still fighting.

"Addie, it's okay. I'm a friend of Astrid's. You call her bumble, right? And she calls you bee."

Recognition cleared the fear from her eyes, and she relaxed into him for a second, the weight of her feeling right in a way he didn't understand.

Her eyes moved back to his, and he waited for her to speak. "You have to help me. Please." Her fingers clawed at him as she tried to sit up.

"What do you need?"

"My daughter. He has my daughter."

Then as if the effort that took was too much, she went slack in his arms, passed out cold, and Lopez felt cold fear crawl up his spine. She had a child, and that child was missing, taken by someone. Even if it killed him, he'd get her back. Anything to take that look of desolation from her stunning face.

A doctor came bustling in moments later with the nurse and asked him to leave so they could examine Adeline. Lopez had no idea why her anguish had affected him as it did and if he were honest with himself, his reason for being by her bedside every chance he got was weak. He told himself it was because he needed the answers he prayed she held, but in truth, it was something about her.

She was beautiful in that effortless way some women were without trying. Petite, barely five foot four, with a slim athletic build, but she had curves where he loved them. Her skin was a similar peaches-and-cream tone as Astrid's but on Adeline, with her dark brown hair, she looked paler, giving her an almost doll-like quality that belied her strength. Her bright green eyes had held him captive for those few seconds and in that time, he feared she could've asked anything of him, and he would've agreed without question.

He paced the hallway, his hand swiping over his slightly longer than normal hair, the curls evident with the longer length. He stopped to remove his glasses, which he only wore when his eyes got tired, and sat on the chair. Her words reverberated around his head. She had a child, a daughter who had been out there this whole time and he'd missed it.

Shame and guilt tore through him and he hated that he'd missed it. He'd been so absorbed with his own search for the truth that he hadn't dived deep enough into Adeline's past. A quick search sure as hell hadn't revealed a child and Astrid never mentioned one.

Taking a deep breath, he pulled out his phone. He had to tell Jack that Adeline was awake. Astrid deserved to know.

"What's wrong?" Jack answered on the second, his no-nonsense greeting to the point.

"Adeline woke up."

Lopez heard the shudder of breath that moved through his boss, the hard man who'd formed Eidolon and led them in every way. Yet Astrid, his now-fiancée, was his weakness, or some might say his strength. He was every bit the hardass he'd always been with his business, and his enemies probably had more to fear than ever before. Once a man had been betrayed like Jack had, nothing else shocked them and mercy became less of a commodity.

His father's betrayal had made Jack strong in a way nobody should ever have to be, and God knew Lopez understood that better than most. It had also made his boss more generous with those he trusted, and he trusted his team.

"We'll be there in twenty minutes."

Jack hung up. Lopez was glad he'd be there when Astrid got the news she was an aunt and that the child she'd known nothing about was missing. If Adeline could be believed she was also in the hands of a man none of them wanted her to be.

His eyes strayed to the door and he wondered what was going on behind it. If she was awake again, if she was okay, or if she was confused. He had the overwhelming compulsion to go to her and hold her hand and tell her she wasn't alone.

The door opened and the doctor came out. Lopez stood to his full height of six foot one. He wasn't built like the rest of the Eidolon crew with bulk and muscle and didn't train with them as often, but he did work out daily and could handle himself. He prided himself on being able to adapt if he was needed. Alex had taught him to fight but Liam had taught him to fight dirty, to play to his strengths, and he was cunning and could read people.

"How is she?"

"We'll run some tests, but she's obviously disoriented still and a little agitated. I've written some medication up for her to help with that and we'll do more when she's had a day or so to rest."

"Can I go back in and see her?"

"Just let the nurses make her more comfortable and you can go in, but she'll need rest and may seem sleepy. Despite what many people think, a coma isn't sleep, and it's not restful. She needs to heal from that."

"Thank you. Astrid is on her way and will likely want to speak with you."

The doctor nodded. "I'll be in my office if she needs me."

The Eidolon men and women had been regulars at the hospital since Adeline was admitted, all of them keeping an eye on Adeline or just wanting to be there for Astrid who was one of the family now.

The nurse who'd first rushed in walked out and held the door for him. "She's awake but sleepy."

Lopez didn't care, he just needed to see she was all right. He caught the door and pushed it slowly open, his eyes on the bed. He was very aware that while he knew her, she didn't know him, and some fear was to be expected after what she'd been through.

He saw her green eyes, startling in their intensity, move to him with caution, her fingers gripping the sheets with nerves.

Lopez held up his hands and moved slow. "Is it okay if I come in and wait until Astrid arrives?"

Her eyes widened and went glossy before she blinked furiously to clear them away. "How...." she began but her throat was croaky from disuse.

Lopez rushed forward and grabbed the water from beside the bed and tilted the straw towards her, his hand cupping her neck to help her. Adeline took a long pull and then another.

"Slow down, you don't want to get sick."

Her eyes moved to his and she let the straw go, a droplet landing on her bottom lip drawing his eyes there.

"How do you know Astrid?"

He could see the suspicion in her eyes and didn't blame her. She didn't know him or anyone here for that matter, and despite her hiding it, he could see her fear. "I work with her fiancé, Jack. Astrid is my friend too."

Adeline's eyes moved over him as if looking for the truth or a lie. "Is she safe?"

"Yes, nobody would dare hurt Astrid on Jack's watch. That man would walk through fire for her."

A smile lit her eyes and then faded. "How long have I been here?"

Lopez sat so he wasn't looming over the bed and making her uncomfortable. He knew the answer to her question would be a blow and would've given anything not to tell her, but he had to. "Five months."

Adeline pushed to try and sit up, her colour draining even more. "Five months. So it's February?"

"March." he corrected, reaching for her hand, and was surprised when she let him help her sit upright. He propped a pillow behind her, and she sighed, as if unaware of her previous discomfort.

"No wonder I feel so weak."

"Your body has been through a lot."

"Where is this place?"

"Beaverbrook is a private facility in Hereford where Astrid and Jack live, and where we're based."

Adeline reached for his hand and gripped it tighter than he thought she could. Electricity zipped along his skin at her innocent touch. He knew she felt it when her eyes flew to his and she snatched her hand away.

"I need to find my daughter."

Her voice was choked as she spoke, and he couldn't imagine how hard it was for her not knowing where her child was. "When Jack and Astrid get here you can tell us everything and we'll get started on looking for her. I promise you, Adeline, we'll get her back."

She shook her head and turned her head toward the wall, a look of hopelessness crossing her face that broke his heart. "You don't know what you're facing."

"No offence but you don't know me, or Eidolon, so don't presume to know what we are and are not capable of."

His words, which he knew were belligerent and antagonistic, did exactly what he'd hoped and sparked a fire in her eyes as they came back to him. He'd rather that any day than the defeat he'd seen seconds ago.

"Then tell me."

"You need to rest, but let's just say we're not your average Black Ops team and we have support from some very well-connected people."

He saw the doubt and didn't blame her, she didn't know him and must be feeling alone and scared and yet she didn't show it. She was a fighter like her sister, but Adeline had so many secrets he wondered if she even knew the truth anymore.

She'd spent so long hiding, could she even be honest and trust them, and if she didn't, could he blame her? How could he when he had his own secrets that half his team didn't know. Some did, like Jack and Decker, but the rest had no idea who his family were or his association with the Ravelino family.

As he looked at Adeline lying on the bed, he knew the time was coming for him to lay all his cards on the table and admit why he'd run from his job at the NSA and joined Eidolon.

The door flew open and brought him out of his reverie. Astrid looked dishevelled and burst into tears the second her eyes landed on her sister.

"Addie. Oh my god, Addie."

Astrid ran to the bed and threw her arms around her older sister, and they clung to each other, holding on tight. Emotion clung to Jack's face as he moved to stand behind the woman he loved, his hand on her back.

Lopez felt like an interloper but couldn't drag his eyes away from the emotional scene. Astrid and Adeline were both crying, and he hated to hear the gut-wrenching pain coming from either woman but something about Adeline's tears gutted him.

Jack must have felt the same because he began to rub soothing circles on Astrid's back. Jack looked across at him, acknowledging him and Lopez dipped his head. He should leave them to it. He was about to leave when the sisters pulled apart.

"Where are you going?"

He looked back at Adeline and saw the panic on her face, a frisson of delight that she wanted him there moved over him and settled into a place in his chest. "I wanted to give you guys some privacy and grab some coffee for everyone."

"Oh my God, coffee. Can I have one?"

Lopez smirked. "I'll check with the nurses and if they say yes, I'll bring you one."

"Thanks."

Lopez winked and walked away whistling, feeling happier than he had in months.

CHAPTER TWO

ADELINE HAD FOUGHT to keep her eyes open after that first emotional outburst when she'd spoken to her sister for the first time in years. Her little Astrid had changed, grown into a strong woman, and had made a life for herself. She couldn't help feeling pride in her sister. So many people had overlooked Astrid, seeing just her beauty, but Adeline had always known that out of the two of them she was the strongest.

Her eyes moved to the man across the room who was hunched awkwardly in a chair, his body at what must have been an uncomfortable angle. His dark brown hair, almost the colour of earth, had fallen over his face. She now knew his name was Javier Lopez but little else, except that he worked for Jack, her sister's fiancé.

Looking across the room she saw Jack was awake and held a sleeping Astrid in his arms, but his eyes were on her. She could feel the way he loved her sister; it was primal in its beauty, and she knew nobody would hurt Astrid while Jack was around. He had a guarded presence about him, as if he too had seen things nobody should.

"You love her very much." Her words were a statement and not a question because any fool could see he worshipped her sister.

His hands tightened around Astrid a fraction before they relaxed again. "She's everything to me."

Adeline tried to sit up, her muscles so weak from months in this bed. The stillness of the early morning gave the room a peaceful feel. "I'm glad, she deserves that."

Adeline felt eyes on her and cocked her head back to the sleeping Javier. His russet brown eyes were assessing her, and she felt a flare of awareness that came out of the blue. It shocked her and made her glance away quickly, the feeling alien to her after so many years of feeling nothing.

A movement had her turning her head again and she saw Astrid climbing off Jack's lap and moving toward her. The big man was watching her, waiting to swoop in and stand between her and anyone who dared upset Astrid, and Adeline knew that was her in this situation.

"How are you feeling?"

Astrid grasped her hand and held tight as if afraid she'd disappear. Adeline would never get over her guilt for what she'd put her family through, but she knew in her heart she'd do it again for Payton. She felt her lip quiver as her thoughts went to her daughter, just four years old and she was God knew where, with someone who didn't have her best interests at heart.

"Hey, what's wrong?" Astrid wrapped her in her arms, and she noticed both and Jack and Javier move in closer, surrounding her like a force of protection.

Her eyes stung with tears, and she blinked them away, trying to get control of her emotions. "I'm sorry, I'm just so worried about Payton."

Adeline glanced up at her sister who looked distraught too. "Tell me everything you can, Addie. We're gonna get my niece back."

Adeline was shocked by the determination in her little sister's voice. She didn't know this Astrid, had never seen her sister look so lethal. "It's a long a sordid story, bumble."

Her sister smiled at her, a breath-taking grin that seemed to light the room with sunshine. "Well, bee, I have nowhere else to be so..." Astrid tipped her hands palm up to the ceiling and shrugged. It was such an Astrid thing to do, that she found herself smiling too.

"Okay."

"Would you like us to leave?"

Javier stepped in closer, brushing his hair from his face in what felt like a nervous gesture. She'd been reading people her whole life and her time in the CIA had made her an expert at watching for signs. Was it possible he was attracted to her? Adeline almost snorted out loud at the ridiculous thought. She probably weighed one hundred pounds soaking wet right now and looked like death warmed up, while he looked like he'd stepped off the cover of GQ or Men's Health. Oh, he didn't have Jack's muscle or bulk, but she could see the corded forearms where he'd rolled up his shirt sleeves, watched the way his biceps flexed when he moved, and knew that under his shirt and the sleepy nerd routine, was a body of steel.

"Adeline?" His voice, which still held a slight Latino accent, was gentle as he said her name.

She shook her head. "No, if you're going to help me, then you need to hear this too."

He gave a terse jerk of his head and pulled up a chair and withdrew his laptop from his bag. Jack and Astrid sat on the other side as they patiently waited for her to tell her story.

She bit her lip, her palms sweaty as she tried to figure out how to tell this story but knew she had to.

Astrid covered her cold hand with her warm one and squeezed gently. "It's okay, Addie, nothing you say in here will shock us and nobody is judging you."

Her eyes flashed to her sister as she swallowed the embarrassment and shame she felt. Even now her sister could read her and understood how she was feeling.

"Let me start at the beginning. When I graduated with my PhD, I had plans to use my degree to study the field of nuclear science in medicine. But almost immediately, I was approached by a man who told me I'd be better served and funded if I worked for them. He gave me a card and told me to call."

"The CIA!" Astrid interjected.

Adeline smiled without humour. "Yes. I called a few days later and they told me I'd be able to use my PhD to work on a program called Maple. It was a classified project involving the use of nuclear energy on tech to scan for viruses. From a medical standpoint, it was extraordinary and could change medicine and how we react to things globally with regard to viruses."

Adeline could feel the ember of excitement in her belly her chosen career used to ignite, as if speaking about it had fanned the ashes into a tiny flame. She sighed, twisting her free hand in the snowy white sheets of her bed. "Anyway, I called and began work. After a year they asked me to go undercover. I'd be trained at the Farm and would be tasked with getting information from Juan Ravelino on his nuclear weapons plans."

Adeline looked around when she thought she heard a growl from Javier who was sitting beside her. His head was buried in his laptop, yet she could tell he was listening, his stillness and the tense set of his body clueing her in.

"Ravelino is an animal. They never should have sent you or Astrid in." Javier was typing as he spoke.

Adeline gasped, her eyes flitting to Astrid. Guilt and pain lanced through her when she saw the truth on her sister's face. "No!"

Astrid squeezed the hand she still held. "It's okay, Adeline. Continue your story and I'll tell mine later."

Adeline struggled to speak, the lump in her throat almost choking her. Javier handed her a glass of water and she took it, thankful for the tiny reprieve. The liquid removed the lump but not the guilt or the anger building like a volcano ready to explode. "I was sent to the town and clubs where Ravelino frequented. My assignment was to get inside his home and get the plans. I caught his eye pretty quickly, but he was shrewd and only entertained me at the club. My handler insisted I do more, give more to get the deal done."

Shame and a feeling of disgust wormed their way through her belly, making the lump in her throat turn to coal. "I felt trapped by then, so I did what they asked. Juan set me up in his home as his mistress and I did everything I could to find the plans until the day I realised I was pregnant."

"Didn't the firm give you the shot? Every female undercover operator gets it."

Adeline didn't want to know how her sister knew that but suspected it was the same reason she did. She saw Jack's hand on Astrid's leg squeeze gently and longed for that kind of faultless support and love, and knew it was a long-forgotten dream. "I did, but I had a short, and what I thought meaningful, relationship with another agent before I went undercover. When he became my handler, he turned cold and made it clear it meant nothing. He's my daughter's father. Anyway, when I realised I was pregnant, I knew I had to get out. Juan was getting increasingly violent. I asked for an extraction and was told no. I called a friend who was the Master Chief for the SEAL team I worked with before going undercover and he pulled me out. We knew I had to die if I wanted to keep my baby safe."

Adeline looked up through blurry eyes as tears burned down her cheeks. "I'm so sorry, Astrid. If there had been any other way, I would've taken it. If I'd come home, I would've put all of you at risk, including Payton, and not just from Ravelino but the firm too."

Astrid rubbed her back, her arm pulling her close as she held her, offering comfort when she was the one who had wronged them all. "It's okay, I would've done the same if the situation was reversed. You're back now and that's what matters. What about Payton, when was she taken and why? Or more importantly by who?"

Adeline pulled away from her sister and took the tissue Javier was holding out to her, wiping her eyes. He'd tilted the lid on his laptop and was watching her carefully, his eyes glinting with anger, and a muscle in his strong jawline twitched.

"About seven months ago she was taken from the day care where we lived in Seward, Resurrection Bay." Adeline looked to Jack, hoping he'd understand why she'd put her sister in danger. "That was when I tried to reach out to Astrid. I had no choice."

His brow creased but he gave her the briefest of smiles. "Was there a ransom?"

"No, nothing but my belief Juan has her and believes she's his child."

"What about the handler?" Astrid crossed her long, elegant legs, biting her lip as she thought. It was a long-remembered trait her sister had. The familiarity of it settled her somehow.

"Joel wouldn't care about a child, he's too busy climbing his way to the top. Or he was the last time I spoke to him when he told me to keep my cover."

"Joel Hansen?"

Adeline's gaze moved to Astrid's face as she heard the shake in her sister's voice. Astrid had gone pale and Jack looked murderous. Adeline had stumbled into something here and she had no clue what it was. "Yes."

"I'm definitely killing that motherfucker." Jack's eyes were flinty cold, the lethal tone nothing compared with the ice that was rolling off his body in tense waves.

"What did I miss?"

"I need a minute." Astrid stood and fled the room, Jack hot on her heels.

Adeline felt abandoned and in the dark like she was watching a movie and had missed an important part. Alone. She felt so alone and then a warm, firm hand closed over her cold fingers and she glanced up to see Javier.

His expression was warm, sympathetic, and she instantly felt less lonely. "What did I say?"

He shook his head as he moved closer to the bed, and she realised he was tall, over six feet and she could feel the warmth from his body, and the lingering scent of his cologne enveloped her, giving her comfort. His thumb rubbed over her knuckles in a soothing circle. She knew she should snatch her hand away and shouldn't allow this comfort from someone she didn't really know but she couldn't seem to do it. She kept her eyes on him and let his touch keep her from falling over the precipice into despair. She was surviving, barely, her fear for Payton a living, breathing leech sucking her will from her, but she had to hang on and not fall apart.

"Astrid was pulled into the CIA after you died." He made air quotes with his free hand. "She was seduced by Hansen too, and even got engaged to him, but he treated her the same way. Left her for dead when her cover was blown. She was beaten and tortured by Juan and Iago for months until she was pulled out."

"Lopez, that's enough." Jack's voice was like a lash in the now silent room.

Adeline slapped a hand over her mouth, trying to hold the sickness at bay. Her bumble had been hurt in ways she'd probably never discuss but she knew. Everything she'd done to keep Astrid safe had failed. In fact, if it wasn't for her, Astrid never would've been there in the first place.

"Oh God, this is all my fault."

"No! Look at me, Adeline."

Her head lifted at Javier's demand as if on autopilot. He looked fierce and angry, but underneath she detected determination.

"This is *not* your fault, stop thinking like a victim. Hansen and Ravelino did this. You were both innocent. I didn't tell you to make you feel guilty, I told you because you needed to know what you're fighting. If you want your daughter back, you need to heal, regain your strength, and then as a team we'll go after them, but you can't do that without the facts."

His speech roused the fire in her, gave her back some of her fight and drive, and she knew as much as his words hurt, they'd help her.

"I want to fight and get my daughter back."

His shoulders went back, his proud chin tilted, and a look of pride moved across his face. She blushed under the feeling, a warmth she hadn't expected seeping into her belly. Suddenly she felt ready to take back her life and had a suspicion this man would be part of that.

CHAPTER THREE

Lopez heard the barking of dogs as he stepped through the back door of Eidolon. He'd barely left his computers these last few days and when he did, he was at Beaverbrook with Adeline, trying to pry more information from her that would help him find her daughter. He'd also tried to give her space to be with Astrid as she underwent tests and got her weak body moving again.

He'd seen the frustration on her face as she fought the weakness months in a bed had caused. He understood it and was pleased to see her courage and fight when she pushed herself to get better. He knew her motivation was the strongest of all, her child and a mother's love.

As the spring sun hit his skin, he turned his head toward the warmth and closed his eyes. The little pleasures in life were something he'd learned to appreciate early. His mother had tried to give him all she could, but money was always tight. Instead, she'd given her time and spent hours talking to him and teaching him things about the world they lived in and the planet they'd leave to the next generation.

He could still remember the lilt of her voice and the smell of her perfume, but it was the feeling of being loved and cherished he remembered most. He missed her every day and wished he could hear her voice giving him advice one more time. Instead, she was gone, and he still had no idea what had happened, but he knew who'd killed her, and the answers lay with Adeline.

Lopez petted Ziggy the Malinois as he trotted over to see him. "Hey, boy, you taking a break from training?"

"Ziggy has an aversion to water. We're trying to train it out of him."

Lopez glanced up as Rafe, the new dog handler, walked toward him. He was Italian and looked every bit the Italian stereotype. Good looking, dark hair, dark brown eyes, and a slim yet muscular build. His English was flawless with almost no accent but then he and his sister Valentina, who was also on the Eidolon team, had grown up in London.

"How are you enjoying it?" Lopez asked.

They'd only spoken a few times, but they'd both seemed nice and watching the brother and sister work together with the dogs was something to behold. They had complete control and the animals seemed to love whatever they were doing, too.

"It's different to what we're used to as far as team dynamic. Val and I have worked together forever but never as part of a bigger team and certainly not one like this, but the work is the same."

"That was a non-answer if ever I heard one."

Rafe laughed and did a hand gesture to make Ziggy sit. "I'm enjoying it a lot but it's a wider dynamic than I'm used to. You guys seem tight."

Lopez shoved his hands in his pockets. "We are but it wasn't immediate. Jack worked us until we became an unbreakable force. I guess that must be intimidating for newcomers."

"A little, but we'll get there, and everyone has been very welcoming."

"A dog unit is something we've needed for a while."

"The set-up you have here is phenomenal."

Lopez looked around and saw Eidolon and the facilities through new eyes for the first time. He was so used to it after five years he didn't always recognise how lucky he was to be there. "Yeah, it is."

"Rafe, stop skiving off."

Lopez and Rafe looked over at his sister Val, who was currently running Ajax and Buddy through the course they'd built since arriving.

Rafe chuckled. "Sisters. Who'd have them."

He turned and waved as he ran back the way he'd come with Ziggy hot on his heels. Lopez watched him give Val a hard time and they broke out in laughter. It was a rare bond they shared, and he wondered what had forged it. He was coming to realise everyone had a story, some were just more tragic than others.

His mind went back to Adeline. He couldn't seem to get his mind off her and found himself thinking of her often and distractedly. He'd known when he'd seen her who she was and how she was linked to him but nobody else did. He also knew she'd lied when she'd told her sister about how she got involved with the CIA and ended up on her first mission.

He knew the truth and wondered why she'd lied or if she'd just forgotten. He didn't see any malice in the lie, but he was intrigued. He'd been searching for answers for so long, yet he'd done everything to distance himself from the stigma of his father's crimes. He'd been tired of dealing with the suspicious looks when people found out who he was, the whispers and the doubt over whether he could be trusted. Everyone bought into the adage the apple didn't fall far from the tree but he knew it wasn't true. He was nothing like his father or at least he didn't think he was. Yet when Adeline had been revealing her story and what she'd suffered, he'd felt like killing them all.

Pushing off the wall he pulled the fire exit door open and walked back inside, the cool air of the building undoing the warmth of the sun and closing out the brightness. It was how he felt around Adeline, as if she were the sun and he was drawn to her warm, bright beauty.

He stopped on his way back to the room he thought of as his war room and grabbed a coffee and two of the dry croissants Alex always made sure were available. Second in command of Eidolon, Alex had wanted to be a chef and was damn good, but life had gotten in the way. Instead, he'd ended up an elite soldier. Losing Evelyn, his childhood sweetheart, had shaped the man he was. Now they were together again and only weeks away from welcoming their first child together.

Lopez passed the gym, hearing the grunts and groans of the men training inside. He poked his head in and was shocked and a little put out to see Adeline standing with Astrid and Jack as they watched Liam and Gunner spar. He stepped forward feeling inordinately annoyed that nobody had told him she was leaving the facility. And why the hell was she there when she should be taking it easy?

Jack turned at his approach, his movements as always sparse, as if he were afraid he'd give something away if he moved quickly. Jack had the best poker face, although nothing like Decker's. "Hey, Lopez, we were just looking for you."

"You found me."

His tone was short, and he knew it hadn't gone unnoticed when Astrid raised a brow. Adeline looked fragile but seeing her in street clothes that hugged the sexy curves she had was like a punch to the balls. Her colour was better, her hair shone, and she looked less like a strong breeze would blow her over. She was still too slim, and it would take a while before she was anywhere near fit enough to take on the fight he knew she'd have to face. The biggest surprise were the sexy freckles that had appeared on her skin, obviously a result of the sun after months inside.

He shoved the croissant in his mouth to stop himself from telling her she looked good and was glad of the coffee in his hand so he didn't do something completely stupid like grab her and pull her to him so he could take a closer look and feel her softness against his own hardness.

"So, uh, what did you want me for?" He chewed and swallowed the dry pastry and kept his eyes off the woman who was wreaking havoc on his senses.

"I know you're busy with all things nerdy, but we wondered if you could show Adeline around and maybe partner with her for some fitness training."

Lopez narrowed his eyes at Jack looking for his angle. There were other people more suited to this than him, but he liked the idea of it being chosen even though it raised his suspicions.

"I can ask Deck if you're too busy."

"No." The word was practically a growl.

He knew when Jack winked at Astrid that he'd been played. Clearly his attraction to, and interest in, Adeline hadn't gone unnoticed, as if he'd be so lucky in a room full of operatives trained to uncover people's secrets. If Jack knew his true intentions though, he'd string him up by his toenails.

Lopez angled his body toward Adeline who was watching silently, but from her expression clearly not missing a thing. "I have time now if you want to see the place, Adeline?"

Her head cocked to the side and he knew she was trying to read him and wondered what she saw. Did she see a good man willing to help a friend or did she see further beneath the skin to the predator underneath?

"Addie. My friends call me Addie."

"Well, Addie, let's go do the tour."

He turned to hide the reaction her smile had on his body and strode for the door. He knew he must look like a rude idiot but better that than her seeing the erection he now had from just the smile she directed his way.

He felt her arm brush his as she jogged to catch up and slowed, feeling like a prick for making her exert herself when she was probably still feeling pretty weak.

"So, you saw the gym, we do a lot of training in there one-on-one and some group sessions. Self-defence, attack drills, and general fitness. Jack makes sure the equipment is top of the range, so we're pretty lucky."

"I'll definitely need to tighten up my training. Those guys back in Montreal handed me my ass."

Lopez stopped walking, fury at what was done to her sparking through his blood. Adeline stopped and glanced at him, uncertainly. "We'll catch those fuckers, Addie, and when we do, they'll wish they'd never been born." He would see to it personally, although he didn't say that.

"I know and thank you, but I need to make sure that I can defend myself and my daughter better. I got sloppy and lazy, and it almost cost me my life and it did cost me my daughter's safety. You guys won't always be around to protect me, so I need to make sure I'm as good as I can be."

Her words niggled at him, and he hated the idea of her not being around or of him not being there when she needed him. Adeline didn't know and neither had he until then, but she was essential to him in a way he hadn't expected. He hardly knew her but after months of sitting by her bed he felt like he did. Lopez kept that quiet. How could he even hope to explain that without sounding like a weirdo and once she knew his plan, she wouldn't want anything to do with him. "Then let's make sure you have all the training you need."

He showed her the kitchen and told her about Alex's coffee obsession and how he liked to cook. He introduced her to Autumn, Maggie, and the newest Eidolon member, Devon who was only six weeks old and according to Mitch, the cutest baby in the world. Lopez took a moment to lavish some kisses on Maggie, who was the princess of the workforce and adored by everyone there. She would soon have playmates in the form of Alex and Evelyn's baby, due any day, and Pax and Blake's baby who was due in a couple of months' time.

Eidolon was exploding with tiny new humans including AJ, Waggs and Willow's son. He wondered who'd be next to pop out a baby and put his money on Liam and Taamira.

He, Decker, Rafe, and Val were the only single ones left and he was curious as to who'd be next to succumb to wedded bliss.

He finished smooching Maggie, making her giggle and reminded Autumn to get herself home before her husband found out she was at work and lost his mind and led Addie away.

Adeline glanced behind her. "That's a sweet set-up Autumn has for the kids."

"Yeah, Jack is all about family. He built most of that himself and plans to extend so we have a full creche facility for the kids."

"Wow, that's above and beyond."

"Maybe, but Jack realises it cuts down on outside factors if his men and their partners are happy, and the happier his men are, the less mistakes happen." He pushed his shoulder against the door to his inner sanctum and faced her. "Plus, if he and Astrid have kids, which depending on which bet you take it is either this year or straight after they get hitched, he'll want Astrid and his baby close. It may have escaped your notice but he's pretty protective of your sister."

"Yeah, I had spotted that, and honestly, I'm so happy she found a man who treats her like she's his whole world. She deserves that, especially after what she went through with Hansen."

He saw the shadow cross her face and wished he could get his hands on the man who'd put that cloud in her eyes. "You do too, Adeline. You were treated horribly, and the CIA should be strung up by their balls for what they put you through."

She shrugged and the gesture made her seem so young, even though she was the same age as he was. "I don't think that's on the cards for me."

"Never say never, Addie. You never know what's around the corner."

"Maybe."

He saw her straighten her spine and force a smile that didn't reach her eyes in any way as she seemed to drag the edges of her fragile psyche around her like a cloak. "Now tell me about this book you have running and how do I get in on that?"

Lopez let her change the subject knowing she needed to focus on something other than herself or she wouldn't get through this. "Step into my office and we'll discuss it."

He held the door open for her and let her duck underneath his arm, her body brushing his and he fought his reaction. Being around her was going to be more difficult than he'd thought. He knew he'd been drawn to her before, felt overprotective but he'd thought it was because of the information she had. Now she was awake, and not just a sleeping beauty but a woman with a personality, he realised he was attracted to her.

Worse, his dick seemed to want action every time she was close and had no decency to the fact she was vulnerable or that it would be an epically bad idea to have sex with Addie. Lopez shook his head and thought of his end game. His erection instantly deflated and guilt he hadn't felt before forced its way to the forefront.

CHAPTER FOUR

TEN DAYS and she still felt as weak as a lamb, her limbs burned and shook as she faced Javier in the ring at Eidolon. Her arms were up, protecting her face, and she bounced on her toes as he smirked and beckoned her with his fingers to attack him. Sweat dripped down her neck and her breathing seesawed but she wouldn't give up.

Adeline had the best reason in the world not to give up, her little girl. She bounced left, mirroring his movements and feigned a high left jab and hit him with an uppercut to the abdomen which he blocked. Lopez might be the geek of the team, but she was learning he was as well trained as the others.

He'd told her his teammates were better and more highly skilled because they had more field training, and perhaps that was true. Nothing counted quite like being in the field, but he was no slouch and probably was technically a better fighter. It didn't matter though; the fact was, he was the only one she felt comfortable enough getting this physical with. The other guys were great and were nothing but nice and sweet to her. It wasn't them; they'd done nothing wrong at all, but she was drawn to Javier. When he touched her, he didn't illicit the fear that was a remnant from her days with Juan.

The last four years had been spent raising her daughter, working as a teacher for the local school, and trying not to do anything to draw attention to herself. She'd dated one guy but there hadn't been any chemistry and he'd only done it to make his ex-wife jealous, which had worked. He'd got back together with her soon after.

"Adeline, focus."

Addie frowned as Javier snapped at her and threw a jab to her head before sweeping her leg out from under her. She found herself on her back with his body pinning hers to the mats. He didn't keep his body there, instantly lifting off her and giving her space. Adeline blew out a frustrated breath and sat up, dropping her arms onto her bent knees.

She hated feeling so weak and pathetic. Astrid had trained with her a little and she was fitter and stronger than she could ever remember her being. Her sister had turned into a warrior or been turned into one by Adeline's actions.

Javier handed her a bottle of water and a small gym towel. "What's going on in that head of yours?"

She took both, wiping the sweat from her face and taking a long drink from the bottle as he watched her, waiting for her answer. "I just feel so pathetic and weak."

"Bullshit, you're neither. You can't expect to wake up after months of being in a coma and expect to be the person you were."

"I bet Astrid would have."

"Is that really what you think?"

Adeline regarded him as he sat next to her before tipping the water up and taking a pull, his Adam's apple bobbing in the strong column of his neck. His dark hair curled wildly around his face before he brushed it back. She had the overwhelming urge to reach out and see if it was as soft as it looked. He was ripped, his arms muscular and strong and his abs the thing dreams were made of, but he didn't have the bulk of the others and she preferred it.

Adeline looked towards the door, wishing someone would walk in so she didn't have to answer that question. Her luck wasn't about to change, and the door remained stubbornly closed. "Astrid has always been stronger than I have."

"She had good people around her, Adeline. She was lucky but you pulled yourself out of that hell and made a new life for yourself and your daughter."

Adeline acknowledged his words, her mind thinking of her bright, funny child. An ache that almost made her double over with pain seared her chest.

"I guess." She sipped her water for something to do to distract herself from the tears that burned her eyes. She wouldn't find her child by crying and moping. She needed to get physically strong first. Her gut instinct was to hop on the first plane to Mexico and storm the Ravelino mansion but that would do nothing except get her killed or tortured, which wouldn't help Payton.

Climbing to her feet, she turned to Javier who was watching her from his seat on the floor, his eyes kind and determined. "Come on, let's do that again and see if I can kick your ass this time."

His smirk was full of confidence which she found sexy, and she reached a hand out for him so he could pull himself up. She grasped his hand, ignoring the zing of awareness that shot through her palm and pulled. He jumped to his feet and took the towel and bottle from her and placed them on the edge of the ring.

It took her five more tries before she eventually managed to execute the move and put him on his back. She had a moments pause and moved to apologise for hurting him or his pride. She'd spent so long deferring to people in the CIA and playing a role but he stopped her with a wide grin.

"That's my girl, you did great. Eventually we'll get you doing this with Jack or Reid or one of the others. They're bigger so it should make it easier, but still, it will require more practice."

"Thanks." Adeline felt a sliver of pride in herself for her achievement, small though it was.

The door to the gym opened and Jack poked his head in. "Do you two have a minute?"

Her heart rate kicked up as she heard the urgency in Jack's voice. "Is something wrong?"

"No, I just want to run something by you both."

"Sure, give me ten minutes to take a shower and change and I'll be there."

Jack nodded once, the movement sparse and controlled, just like the man himself. He was different at home with Astrid. More relaxed, still dominant, but not an asshole. Since her release from Beaverbrook, she'd seen first-hand how they were together. Moving in with a newly engaged couple was awkward to say the least. They were always touching and kissing, and she knew they tried to keep the noise down, but it was clear they had a very active sex life, and she hated that she was stifling that for them.

She needed her own space while she was there. Perhaps she would ask Javier about it, see if he knew anyone with an apartment to rent. Adeline walked to the edge of the boxing ring, and Javier reached up a hand to help her jump down. She hesitated just a fraction and he raised an eyebrow, telling her without words to stop being ridiculous.

"I'll see you in there."

"Okay."

Adeline rushed through her shower when she would have liked to luxuriate in it. She tied her long, wet hair into a simple ponytail and shoved her legs into purple yoga pants and pulled on a black, scoop neck t-shirt. She wore running shoes and a hoodie, the cold of the early spring in the UK making her shiver.

Eidolon had become familiar to her over the weeks. She walked down the hallway past Autumn's empty office and the sweet smells from the break room to the tech room, where she'd spent most of her time with Javier looking for leads.

When she entered, she saw Jack, Astrid, Javier, and Alex already seated around the monitors.

"So, what's up?" She moved to stand beside Astrid, her sister taking her hand as she often did, and Adeline knew it was to reassure herself that she was alive, and it wasn't all a dream. She hated knowing she'd done that to her sister. She also knew she had to face a reunion with her parents at some point but had begged Astrid to keep her secret until she had Payton back safe.

Jack looked up at her. "What I say next doesn't leave this room. Only a handful of people know what I'm about to tell you."

He waited for her assent, and she crossed her arms. "Of course. You have my word."

Jack seemed to think that was enough. "Eidolon has a second team, called Shadow Elite. While Eidolon is a ghost ops team, we still have to obey certain restrictions. Shadow is completely dark and doesn't exist anywhere on paper. Most of the members left behind their lives to be part of the team."

Adeline still didn't know what this had to do with her and shifted from foot to foot impatiently while she waited.

"I have three members of Shadow on their way to Mexico to stake out the Ravelino mansion. They know us, but they don't know Shadow. Duchess, Bás, and Bein are already en-route to get us intel on the ground and to get eyes on Payton."

Adeline felt her chest tighten and her heart began to race at the thought of people putting themselves in danger, and she knew more than most how dangerous the Ravelino cartel were. Yet, she also felt a huge amount of relief to know there were friendlies finally close to her daughter.

"How sure are you that Ravelino has her? Could it be Hansen for some unknown reason?"

Adeline shook her head. "I don't know for sure, but my gut says they have her. He'll use her to make me finish what I started, plus me taking what he perceives as his will be a slight he won't let go of."

Astrid squeezed her hand in support. "That ties into what I know of him, too."

"Our intel says Ravelino is looking for a new scientist after he had the last one killed for making a mistake, so I agree he'll use Payton to draw Adeline out." Lopez was looking at her as he spoke, his hair still wet from his shower.

"But that doesn't tie in with you getting beaten." Alex folded his arms over his chest and discreetly checked his watch. She knew he was on constant watch for a call from Evelyn that she was in labour. The man was a wreck worrying about her and Adeline liked him even more for it. "Could that be Hansen's doing?"

Adeline shrugged. "I guess. The CIA won't want me alive after I ran, I know too much. I'm surprised Astrid is safe to live her life here."

Jack frowned. "Astrid has protection of a different kind and so will you. Nobody would dare to touch her, not even the firm."

Adeline dipped her head so as not to show how much being included in this family of theirs meant to her. "Thank you."

"Not a problem. You're one of us now, Adeline, and we take care of our own."

Adeline could see why her sister had fallen in love with this man. If she were anyone else, she'd be swooning right about now, but she was too worried for her daughter. She needed her safe and in her arms again.

CHAPTER FIVE

THE WHIR of the fans on his multiple computers was the only sound in the room. Lopez stretched his arms over his head, trying to rid his body of the kinks that sitting in a chair hunched over a screen for hours had given him. He'd been looking into cases that Joel Hansen had handled. Hours of time spent learning from the best hacker in the world and one of his bosses, Will Granger, had been put to good use.

Hacking the CIA was risky, they weren't known for being lenient and were by far the shadiest of the alphabet agencies. But so far, he'd managed to get in and out without triggering any alerts. He ran his eyes over one redacted file after another, gleaning snippets of information but not enough to help him.

What he'd learned was that Hansen was a complete asshole. He used whomever he thought could further his career and Adeline and Astrid hadn't been the only women he'd slept with and lied to. The man was a leech, sucking the hard work of others and using it to further his own career. He'd found at least two complaints from other women about sexual misconduct, but they'd been buried, and Lopez wanted to know why. Someone had this guy's back, and whoever it was had power and influence behind them.

He glanced up, his eyes gritty from so much screen time. He knew he'd need to put his glasses on or risk a headache and he had too much work to do to stop for a headache. He pulled them out of the drawer and was putting them on when the door opened.

He smiled when he saw Adeline, before glancing at the clock. "You're here late."

She had two Styrofoam containers in her hand. He got a whiff of whatever she was carrying, and his belly rumbled, reminding him it was way after dinner and he hadn't eaten. That was usual for him. He often got so involved with what he was doing he lost all track of time.

"I never left. I wanted to stay and practice some of the moves you taught me." She placed the container beside him. "I guess you haven't eaten yet if the way you're staring at that is anything to go by."

Lopez smirked. "You got me."

Adeline pushed it closer. "Astrid made Jack bring it over when I said I was going to stay and work on some leads. I hope you like burgers."

Lopez opened it and saw his favourite bacon burger with loaded fries and groaned. "You're a goddess."

Adeline laughed as she pulled a chair close beside him and sat. He could smell her body wash through the smell of the greasy burger. He began to eat, the flavours bursting on his tongue as the grease and juice dribbled down his chin. He swiped at it with a napkin and swallowed. They ate in silence for a bit, both lost in their food, and he was amazed at how companionable it was.

He pushed the empty container away, and put her finished meal on top, ready to take them to the bin outside later. The last thing he wanted was his workspace smelling like a takeaway diner.

"So, Hansen is a douche canoe."

Adeline gave a derisive laugh. "Yep, he is. Thank God Payton didn't get a single trait from him."

"He has two sexual misconduct claims on his file, but both were quashed. It looks like he makes a habit of manipulating female operators and using their hard work to further his career. He's also lost three assets in the field, you, Astrid, and a man only referred to as Agent P. Yet he still seems to come out looking lily-white and with his reputation, at least among the brass, squeaky clean. How is that possible?"

"He's distantly related to Jim Baker. I think he's his wife's second cousin."

Lopez sat forward so fast the wheels on his chair skidded. "The director of the CIA?"

"Yes, the one and only."

"Well, that explains why he gets away with the shit he does."

"Nobody likes Hansen, but I was foolish, and he was charming."

Lopez saw the blush spread across her cheeks as she dipped her head. He wondered how she had managed to do the job she'd been shoehorned into. Adeline wasn't cut out for the world of espionage, not like Astrid was. Adeline was gentle, her hard edges honed from fear not natural ability. She'd done well to have gotten as far as she had but she was always going to get burned, because she lacked the edge needed for the work.

It made him irrationally angry that they'd put her in that position and basically used her as if she was expendable. She was strong, because she'd had no choice and so damn brave, but the point was, she shouldn't have had to change who she was when what he saw of her nature was so damn perfect.

"Don't apologise for being sucked in by him, Adeline. We've all got that one person in our past who fooled us. At least you have your daughter to show for it, so you win, right."

"I guess so and I wouldn't change a thing about her. She's everything that is good in the world."

Her eyes literally lit up when she spoke of Payton, he could feel the love she had for her child from across the room and it reminded him of his mother. She was utterly stunning but even that word didn't describe the beauty of her love for her little girl. "She sounds amazing."

"She is. She loves art and drawing and is learning to play the piano." Adeline was smiling now, lost in her thoughts. She tucked her hands between her thighs and hunched forward, looking up as if seeing the memories in her head. "She likes to bake and loves sushi."

"Really? Wow, that's unusual, isn't it?"

Adeline chuckled. "Yeah, she's years ahead of herself. She can read some of the first-grade books already and adores nature."

"Do you have a picture?" Lopez had the sudden desire to put a face to this child and not the one Shadow had, which was a simple headshot, but an image captured by her mother.

"Yes, but I need to get into my cloud to find it."

Lopez scooted back out of the way so she could load her cloud drive. He watched her as she typed, seeing the colour coming back to her skin with her renewed health and it made him happy to see her alive and fighting.

"Here you go."

She turned just as he leaned closer to get a look, his breath skimming her bare shoulder where her tank top ended. A ripple of goosebumps flew over her skin, and he saw awareness creep into her eyes. His breath caught and she seemed to still, as if waiting for his next move. The room was silent except for the machines, and he had the overwhelming urge to kiss her. To taste those pouty pink lips and find out if her skin was as soft as he imagined.

A pulse fluttered in her neck, and she swallowed slowly as if afraid to break the moment. Lopez had never wanted anything more. Seeing this sweet, gentle woman and hearing of her love for her child, he'd seen the life she'd made for them both. The risks she'd taken and the bravery and courage that had been used against her by unscrupulous people and he wanted that. He wanted her in a way he didn't understand and couldn't begin to explain, and that made him a grade-A bastard because he was as bad as the rest of them.

Lopez blinked and pulled away, breaking the spell as he turned to the computer screen. "Wow, she's a cutie. She looks a lot like Astrid, but she has your eyes."

"Yeah, she's a lot like my sister. She has a fire in her belly."

Lopez felt the food in his belly turn to acid as she shared her daughter's life with him. He tried to tell himself he didn't care but he did. He wanted the answers to where his mother's body was buried, and Adeline was the key. She was the woman who'd helped bring down his father thanks to the intel she'd passed on to Hansen while she was under cover at the Ravelino mansion. The same hitman who'd done the dirty work for Juan and Iago and murdered his mother.

He shook the thoughts away and focused on Adeline as she spoke, trying to concentrate on her words.

"Thank you for helping me, Javier, I don't know what I would've done without all of you."

He felt like a fraud accepting her thanks but what else could he do? The team had no idea about his personal mission. They were helping because they were good men and as Jack had said, Adeline was family now. He would've felt the same but now his feelings were mixed up with self-hatred for lying to her and his friends.

After Gunner, there'd been a rule about this kind of shit. Gunner had been vulnerable because he'd kept secrets and it had almost destroyed the team. Now he was doing the same thing. He needed to tell Jack how involved he was with this before he put everyone at risk. Yet the closure of knowing where his mother's body was buried was something he needed to move on with his life.

"It's fine. Now tell me about the SEAL team who helped you escape initially. Why didn't you ask them for help?"

He could tell he'd stunned her with his sudden change in direction, but she brushed it off and he kept his face friendly but neutral. He couldn't let her get close to him and hurt her, no matter how much he craved her touch.

"Um, well, they're away on a mission and I can't reach them, or I couldn't when Payton was taken. I haven't reached out since I woke.

They're all still active duty and they risked enough to pull me out. I won't ask for more when I already have help. They mean too much to me."

Lopez felt an uncomfortable annoyance at her obvious affection for the men who'd saved her and realised it was jealousy. He crushed the feeling under his boot, disgusted with his inability to stay remote with Adeline. "Makes sense. So as soon as we have active intel, we'll move. Shadow is out of my control. I don't have access to that team or any real knowledge about them either."

"So, I guess we just wait and keep digging for as much intel as we can until then."

"Are you going to the Easter Egg hunt on Sunday with Astrid and Jack?"

Adeline twisted the hem of her top in her fingers before she looked up and he saw the hesitancy. "I guess."

"Don't want to go?"

She shrugged. "I just feel guilty doing anything like that when Payton is missing."

"I get that, but the alternative is you sit at home alone and stew in guilt and what-ifs."

"I know and I'll go because Astrid is so excited about it. She wants me to meet all her friends. Will you be going?"

"Yes, we all go. It's become something of a tradition for Zack Cunningham from Fortis to host these things. He has a country Estate which is huge, and the grounds are beautiful and vast."

"Yeah, Jack's cousin Jace works for them. Astrid was telling me about them all."

"Yeah, they help us out from time to time and we help them. They've become extended family and friends."

"It sounds like a perfect set-up and a wonderful life. I'm happy Astrid has that."

"Maybe you can have it too one day, when you get Payton back. Jack will make sure you're safe to live your life and you won't have to hide. You can stay here with your sister and get your family back. I know she'd love that."

"I would too, but I can't think about any of that until I get Payton back. Everything else is unimportant until she's safe."

"I understand." He did and yet her avoidance of an answer sat like lead in his belly. He realised he wanted her to stay and yet that was perverse when she'd eventually hate him for lying to her.

His feelings for Adeline were becoming more and more complex by the second and becoming tangled up in his lies and omissions. He had no right to want her like he did, but his body didn't seem to get the memo. He didn't know exactly what it was about this woman that snared his attention.

He'd been working around beautiful, confident women for years. Some more beautiful and definitely more confident. Zenobi for a start —all of them were knock-your-socks-off stunning. The women his friends loved, like Cassie, Taamira, Lacey, and Willow were again gorgeous. Two were models for God's sake but they'd never affected him like Adeline did. It was a cruel trick of nature that the woman he had to hurt and lie to was the one who took his breath away with her gentle beauty.

Adeline began to pack up the containers and he switched off the computers. He'd take his laptop home and connect it to his set-up there. He swung his laptop bag over his shoulder and walked her to the door, keeping his eyes above the sweet curve of her butt. "You need a lift home?"

"Nah, Jack is in his office and said to find him when I was done."

He stopped at the door, listening as the building settled into silence. "Well, I'll see you Sunday."

She turned away and walked before twisting back around. "See you Sunday, Javier."

He grinned at her use of his given name. She was the only person who called him that and he liked it. Once again he realised how screwed he was.

CHAPTER SIX

Adeline felt slightly out of her comfort zone being around so many people she didn't know, but who obviously knew about her. It made her feel like a bug under a microscope. The slight breeze kicked her dark hair into her face, and she reached up to tuck a strand behind her ear, her gaze moving around the beautiful gardens.

The weather was good for this time of year with the sun making a break through the clouds. It felt wonderful to feel the warmth on her skin. She'd never got used to the cold of Alaska and tipped her face to the sun, closing her eyes for a beat to just enjoy it.

Her eyes sprung open, the ache of the loss she experienced at the thought of her daughter almost crippling her. She sucked in a deep breath, willing the panic she felt squeezing her chest away and controlling her oxygen intake, so she didn't make a fool of herself.

The Cunningham Estate was just as Javier had said, with large trees around the periphery and a huge, landscaped garden with a massive lawn where children were currently running around. They seemed to vary in age from babies in their parents' arms to young teens.

Astrid looped an arm through hers and laughed, the sound light and free as she too watched them. Had she ever been that free? It was hard to remember a time when her life had been her own. Even as a youngster she'd felt the pressure to do well, to make use of the brain God had given her. She was the bright one, the one who studied hard and got the best grades. She loved her studies, she couldn't deny that, but she'd never felt free.

"I'm so happy you're here."

Adeline smiled up at Astrid who was wearing a long, cream floaty skirt and pale green shell top with a denim jacket over the top. Adeline was wearing khaki fitted trousers and a navy blouse with trainers, and as usual, felt like she'd just missed the mark. Astrid looked trendy and happy, and Adeline felt a rush of love for her baby sister. Astrid was the only one who'd ever seen past her brains to the fun person hiding beneath.

"Me too. I missed you so much. Payton is so much like you that sometimes it hurt to think of you."

Astrid turned to face her as they stopped near a group of women drinking wine as they sliced an array of cakes and wrote names on small, decorated baskets.

"We'll get her back, Addie. We won't stop until she's home and I can show her that I'm the best damn aunt ever. She needs to be my flower girl and I won't get married without her."

Adeline felt her eyes sting with tears at her sister's forthright declaration. She took a calming breath to get her emotions under control and changed the subject. "I spy cake."

Astrid watched her for a few more seconds, as if making her own assessment of Adeline's mental wellbeing. "Well, let's get some cake before the men descend and eat it all."

She looped her arm back through her sister's and walked to the group of women.

"Ladies, this is my sister Adeline."

Adeline regarded the women, some she'd met already. Roz, Evelyn, who looked ready to burst as her pregnancy neared the end, and Pax, who had the tiniest, neat bump it was hard to believe she was seven months pregnant. Adeline had met all the wives and girl-friends, or wags as they called themselves to piss the real Waggs off, of the Eidolon men. They were frequent visitors at their husbands' place of work. Autumn was chatting with Princess Taamira, who Adeline had thought was the most beautiful woman she'd ever met and then she'd met Cassie and Lacey, who were just as stunning. Willow smiled shyly but it was genuine and she wondered if she felt as intimidated by all these stunning beauties as she did, although Willow was just as beautiful in her opinion.

It stood to reason that gorgeous men like the ones that worked for the ghost ops company would attract equally attractive partners. Although none of them seemed to be aware of just how good looking they were, not the men or women. It made her think of Javier Lopez. She'd been sure he was going to kiss her the other night, and despite it being an epically bad idea she'd wanted him to kiss her. Thankfully, he'd had some sense and had broken the spell that had seemed to fall over them in the quiet room.

Javier was handsome and sexy, and had a body made for sex. He should be on book covers and when he added those sexy glasses, it was all she could do to get her words out. She'd never been a femme fatale around men, by nature she was shy and reserved. Her training with the CIA had helped her act out her role but when she was being plain old Adeline Lasson, she was as far from a sex kitten as cheese was to a sweet. Which was a million miles away. Whoever had decided cheesecake was a good idea needed shooting as far as she was concerned.

Lacey was sitting next to a dark-haired woman she didn't know, and she caught Adeline's eyes and smiled, holding out her hand. "Skye, nice to meet you."

Adeline shook her hand and smiled. "You, too."

Skye shuffled over in her seat making room for her. "It can be pretty overwhelming, can't it?"

Astrid patted her hand and Adeline turned. "I have to go rescue Jace from Jack. He's trying to steal Harlow for the easter egg hunt."

Adeline's gaze followed Astrid's and she saw Jack with a baby around six months old in his arms, facing an equally determined man who wanted his child back. It looked hilarious and she chuckled. "Better go do that before war breaks out."

Adeline sat beside Skye who was writing the name Noah on a basket.

Adeline waved her hand around the gardens. "So, which one of these is yours?"

Skye snorted. "The one over there being used as a jungle gym by his daughter."

Adeline glanced at a large, dark-haired man with a little girl on his shoulders talking to Javier, who was holding Maggie. Her breath caught and it had nothing to do with the handsome man Skye had pointed out and everything to do with Javier. His wavy hair was tousled from the small child who was absentmindedly stroking her small hand through it, and he looked calm, relaxed, and somehow familiar in a way she couldn't place. Like she knew him or at least her body seemed to. Her skin prickled with awareness, and as if sensing her watching, he turned and smiled, his eyes lighting up with warmth and desire.

"Lopez is cute, right?"

Adeline startled out of her ogling of the sexy man and blushed as she turned back to Skye with guilt in her eyes. "You must think I'm awful lusting after a man when my child is missing." She felt like a disgusting human being for even thinking about sex or desire.

Skye tipped her head; a kind look on her face. "Not at all. Nate and I got together when Noah was missing. His father kidnapped him for his own selfish reasons, which I won't go into now, but it threw Nate and I together and I wouldn't have got through it without him. He was the rock I needed that stopped me from completely falling apart." Skye gently touched her arm. "I know you don't know me, but I know what you're going through and if you need a shoulder to cry on or someone to talk to, then call me. Having a child go missing is every parent's nightmare and there's no set way to get through it. You just do the best you can and lean on those you trust in whatever form that takes."

"Wow, I had no idea."

"It was a few years ago and I still wake up in a cold sweat over it. I think I always will. You don't forget a trauma like that, but if anyone can get her back to you it's these men and women here today. There's nobody better or more invested."

Adeline turned back to Javier who was walking toward her, having given Maggie over to her father.

"Just have faith, Adeline, and if you need me, call me. Lopez has my number."

Adeline faced the woman who seemed to know exactly how she felt and held no judgement for her losing her child. "Thank you."

Skye patted her arm. "Now, let's get these baskets handed out so this egg hunt can begin. Honestly, I don't know who's more competitive, the kids or the men."

"Hey."

Javier was standing with his hands in his pockets looking sexy as hell in a white polo which showed off the gorgeous tone of his skin, and had a devilish smirk on his face she wasn't even sure he knew he wore. Her body responded to him, her words fumbling in her brain without a single touch. What would it be like to feel his hands on her, to feel alive again? She was getting her strength and fitness back, and the rest of her long-buried emotions were waking with it.

"Hey, you're not taking part in the egg hunt?"

Javier looked out at where everyone was gathered accepting baskets and rallying their kids and smirked. "Um, no. I'll leave that to the dads and the over-sized children I call my colleagues."

She looked to where Liam and Gunner were fighting over a small boy who they'd decided needed their help and laughed as another man with a slight limp swooped in and snatched the child away.

The two looked outraged and she laughed loudly, her hand covering her mouth.

"That was Drew, and the boy is his nephew Aaron. Drew is a techy like me, although he works out like a machine."

"Yeah, he looks like he could bench press a car."

"He stays in shape so he probably can. You want to take a walk?"

Adeline shrugged. "Sure, sounds nice."

Javier led her towards the other side of the huge garden as they strolled in an amicable silence past daffodils, snowdrops, and purple grape hyacinth. It was peaceful and made even more perfect by the distant laughter and joy she could hear from the egg hunt behind them.

"It's beautiful here."

Javier studied her, the sun catching his hair and making the dark strands glint with gold. "It is and you should see this place in the summer. Zack and Ava always throw a summer barbecue and have a bouncy castle for the kids. Maybe you can bring Payton to meet the other kids."

Her heart clenched and she stopped walking. Javier stopped and cursed as he walked back to her. He slid his arms around her gently, not forcing his hold on her and she grasped his shirt in her fingers, holding on tight.

"Damn, Addie, I'm sorry. That was insensitive of me. I didn't mean to upset you."

She could feel his hands stroking her hair, his warm body against hers, the thud of his heart and the genuine remorse in his words. No tears came but the sense of loss was a constant ache and the fear that cramped her stomach was almost the norm for her now.

"I just don't know how to breathe without her. I feel like I'm one second away from falling apart all the time."

Adeline felt his lips on her hair and closed her eyes, the scent of woodsy spice and sandalwood mixed with a clean mountain-fresh scent filled her nose and made her want to sniff him. She felt safe in his arms from the buffeting guilt and despair.

Lifting her head, she saw worry in his eyes but as she held his gaze, her breathing becoming fast, his dark gaze became sensual and full of the desire she felt pooling in her belly.

"Tell me to stop, Addie."

His breath feathered against her skin, and she lifted up on tiptoes, her hands moving over his chest, and she felt him grasping for control as it began to slip. "No."

His lips crashed into hers and it was heat and need, his lips firm and soft as he stroked his tongue against the seam of her lips. Addie thrust her fingers into his silky hair and he growled, the sound sexy as hell. He nipped her lip then soothed it with his tongue, a whimper of pleasure slipping from her throat as his hands pulled her closer to his hard body.

Her head fell sideways as his lips moved over her cheek and down her neck, nipping at her pulse with his teeth as she pulled his hair. Her body seemed to move of its own accord, her hips rocking against his erection that pressed into her belly.

Suddenly he pulled his mouth away, his hands cupping her face, the unchecked need in his face heady and sexy. "Fuck, Addie, you make me forget my own name."

"I want you, Javier. Make me feel alive."

She could see the battle wage on his expressive face, the need fighting with his sense of right. "Not like this, not on the cold ground with your family mere feet away. If you want this then we slow it down. I won't fuck you like an animal."

Adeline pulled away, letting his hands fall from her heated skin. "I don't want more. I can't offer you anything else, Javier."

"I'm not asking for a commitment, Addie, but I won't treat you like a whore either."

Addie rounded on him. "You think fucking in the open is treating me like a whore?"

He gentled his tone, even as he scowled. "No, of course not, but if we have sex, I want it to be because you want it, not to block the pain and grief you're feeling, and not with lies between us."

Her fight left her at his honesty, and she knew he was right. It would just be an escape and she knew she'd regret it afterwards and she didn't want that. He was right, she wasn't this woman, but it just hurt so bad, and she wanted the hole in her heart gone.

Javier walked toward her and took her hand, bringing it to his lips. "I wish I could take this from you, to carry your heartache but I can't." His lips touched her knuckles and she blinked back the tears that threatened. "How about I be your friend and if you decide you want more after thinking about things, then let me know."

Addie was grateful he'd put the brakes on things, she would've slept with him without thought and regretted it, feeling like the slut they'd called her. She didn't have mindless sex with people she hardly knew, although the alternative had hardly been a success either.

"Thank you, Javier, for being a good man."

She saw him wince, but it was gone before she could question it. "How about we go and get some cake and find out which of the big kids won the Easter egg hunt."

She smiled. "Okay."

He kept a foot of distance between them on the walk back and she missed the easy friendship they'd struck up already.

CHAPTER SEVEN

He had to get the fuck out of there before he did something they'd both regret, like drag her behind the closest locked door and fuck her until neither of them could speak. His body tightened as he watched her smile at Liam and Alex, a wave of jealousy that was completely unwarranted suffusing his body.

He spun on his heel. He had to leave, now. As he walked to his car, he dialled Decker. His friend avoided events like this like the plague and he wondered if he wanted to grab a beer. "Hey, Deck."

"Hi. You had enough of chocolate already?"

"Something like that. Wanna grab a beer?"

"Sure, sounds like a plan. The usual or do you want to go someplace else?"

"How about The Grapes? It has a pool table."

"Sure. See you in about twenty minutes, get a round in."

Lopez smirked. He always got the first round in. "Sure."

He hung up and drove the fifteen minutes into town, parking by the river and walking briskly toward The Grapes Tavern. The bar was dark, the lighting low but classy with sconces on the walls and a long walnut bar with brass taps and sparkling optics. He sat on a stool as he ordered two pints of Guinness and paid. He was just taking the first sip of his drink when Decker walked in and spotted him.

He walked straight over and took a seat beside him, grasping his beer and taking a long pull before sighing and placing it back on the bar. "Wanna get a table?"

Lopez looked around and noticed a table near the back and nodded.

The two men sat, and Lopez looked at Decker. He was wearing a navy suit with a white shirt, his only concession to casual his open collar. "Do you sleep in a fucking suit?"

Decker stopped with his pint halfway to his lips and then smirked. "Gee, Lopez, I didn't know you cared."

"Asshole."

"How about instead of trading insults you tell me what's really bothering you?"

Lopez frowned, he wasn't in the mood to be analysed by Decker or anyone else. "Nothing's bothering me."

Decker quirked a brow. "Uh-huh."

"What the fuck does that mean?"

Deck took a slow sip of his beer and Lopez struggled not to lose his temper.

"Just that you spent the best part of three months sitting at Adeline's bedside like a lovesick puppy and now you look at her like you want to jump her bones."

Lopez groaned. "I'm fucked, Deck. I knew she was beautiful, any idiot with eyes can see that but I like her. She's sweet and determined and so damn strong and she's hurting so bad."

"And you're worried you're going to hurt her because when she finds out who you are and what you're hiding, she'll hate you for lying to her?"

Lopez should have known Decker would see right to the heart of things and not pull his punches. It was one of the things he liked most about his friend, his straight-talking. It was also supremely annoying sometimes. "Pretty much." He swiped at the drop of condensation on his glass. "If I tell her I'm the son of the Ravelino Cartel's hitman, the same hitman she helped put away and ask for her help to find out what happened to my mother, then she's going to think she can't trust me, and I lose any chance of finding out if this connection is real."

"But you get closure about your mother's death."

"Exactly, *if* she's willing to help me. If I don't tell her and she finds out, then she'll hate me for lying to her."

"So be honest. Tell her about your past and that you realised who she was and wanted her help but hadn't counted on falling for her."

Lopez lifted his head quickly. "I'm not falling for her. I hardly know her."

"Oh, please. You spent months at her bedside and every spare second helping her. Lie to yourself, Lopez, but not to me."

"When did you realise who she was?"

Lopez wasn't sure how Deck knew about Adeline being the CIA operator who'd helped bring down his father before she'd been picked to go undercover. He only knew because of some very illegal hacking he'd done, and he was damn lucky not to have gotten caught.

"I caught your reaction to her name in Canada and did some digging."

Lopez looked down at the beer mat with the name of the local brewery on it. "Does Jack know?"

Decker shook his head as he placed his glass back on the table. "No, but you need to tell him. Secrets nearly destroyed us once before and he's invested in this. She's going to be his family and if you fuck this up, he won't be happy."

Lopez snorted at that. Jack would be fucking livid if Lopez hurt Adeline. He was ridiculously protective of Astrid and he'd go mad if she was upset. He even walked that fucking tiny dog Cupid on a lead around the compound because Astrid worried the other dogs might hurt the little shit. He looked ridiculous but it also made Lopez smile to know that a man like Jack could put aside his pride and feelings for the woman he loved.

"I'll talk to him tonight and explain and hope he doesn't ask Shadow to bury me where my body will never be found."

Decker chuckled. "Yeah, and it wouldn't be. Those guys don't fuck around."

"What do you know about them?"

Lopez knew he could talk to Decker about the secret group because Jack had told him Decker knew and that he'd done the evaluations on each team member.

"Some interesting characters for sure, but they're all focused and deadly and ready to colour outside the lines if need be to get the job done."

"Let's hope they can get a lead on Payton."

"If she's there, they'll find her."

Lopez saw the current players hand their cues back and nodded at the empty table. "Fancy a game of pool?"

"Sure, if you don't mind losing."

Decker removed his jacket and hung it over the back of his chair, before rolling up his sleeves. Lopez saw a few women at the bar watching his friend, but Decker seemed not to notice.

Lopez began racking the balls and waited for Decker to break. The sound of the game and the clink of glasses and chatter relaxing him slightly.

"So, what will you do?" Decker was chalking his cue as he asked the apparently innocent question.

Lopez sighed as he took his shot, sinking the purple in the top left corner of the pocket. "No fucking clue. But I've been searching for answers to my mother's death for so long, I don't think I can give it up."

"But?"

Fucking Decker. "But I can't stop thinking about her. I fucking kissed her this morning and I can't get it out of my mind."

"Well, you need to figure it out. She's been through enough without you adding to her heartache and I suggest you keep your dick in your pants until you do, or Jack is going to chop it off."

Lopez straightened and shot Decker a filthy look. "I fucking know that. I need to stay away from her and find the answers, Deck. I need to know if my father killed my mother and where her body is. I need to lay her to rest."

"I understand that."

"I know you do." Decker had suffered his own tragedy and never really talked about it. Sometimes Lopez wondered what would happen if Decker ever allowed himself to let go. "I just never imagined myself wanting to be with someone like I do her. I was always happy with the life I had here. I hated my life at the NSA, always having people looking at me with suspicion when they found out who my father was. With doubt in their eyes as to whether I was like him in some way and whether the apple had fallen far from the tree. I hated it. Then Jack offered me this job and gave me purpose. I made a new life for myself, but my driving force has always been to find the truth and now I don't know what the fuck to do. I need the truth but I'm not sure I want to walk away from her either."

"How does she feel?"

"No fucking clue. As I said, it was one kiss and some sexual tension. I stopped it before it went further. She is hurting and I don't want her to do anything she'll regret."

Decker leaned down and potted the black off the cushion. "Sounds like more than attraction, seems like you care."

Lopez swept his hand through his hair and picked up his pint, downing the last dregs and wiping the foam from his mouth. "I'm not an asshole and I do care. She's a nice woman, devoted to her child, cute as fuck, and feisty as hell."

"You should tell her the truth. But whatever you decide, you need to tell Jack."

"Or?" Lopez challenged, feeling short-tempered and backed into a corner of his own making.

Decker watched him for a second his face impassive. "Or nothing. This is your decision, Lopez."

Lopez felt his fight leave him; his friend wasn't giving him an ulti-matum just advice, which Lopez realised was why he'd called him.

"Do you miss it? Being part of a couple?" He'd never asked Decker before, had never really considered it but he felt himself wanting that now. Not necessarily because of his attraction to Adeline but to be part of something like his friends were.

"Every. Fucking. Day."

Lopez looked up at Decker whose voice was raspy and saw a glimpse of the grief he carried with him and rarely showed. He was showing it now and it almost gutted Lopez to see that kind of pain. Decker blinked and it was gone, shuttered once again behind the walls his friend kept up.

"Would you ever re-marry?"

Decker shook his head emphatically. "No, I loved my wife, and my children were my world. I'll never regret a single day with them, but I won't allow myself to be that vulnerable ever again. I wouldn't survive it twice. I barely survived the first loss."

It was the most open Lopez had ever seen him and showed a wound that was far from healed. "I'm here if you ever want to talk, Deck."

Decker nodded shortly. "Now, I guess it's my round. Wanna grab some food and I'll give you a chance to redeem yourself after this embarrassing display?"

Lopez looked at the table and saw he'd been seven balled while he'd contemplated his choices. "Yeah, sure, and this time you're gonna get your ass handed to you."

"Dream on, Lopez. Dream on."

Lopez watched his friend go to the bar and order two more drinks and grab a couple of menus. Decker was right, he needed to tell Jack and Adeline the truth. He had no clue if this deep-seated need to be with Adeline was real or based on their unknown but shared history, or if it was simply a sexual attraction they needed to get out of their systems. But she deserved the truth either way, and he'd give her that and face the consequences.

CHAPTER EIGHT

"Are you sure this is okay? I can stay back at your place and get some reading done. I don't want to intrude on family time."

Astrid arched one of her perfect brows and Jack chuckled from the front seat. "When are you going to clue in, Adeline, that as far as I'm concerned, you're family. You're going to be my sister-in-law and my mother is beyond happy to have another woman on her side after years of just men in her house." He took Astrid's hand and kissed her knuckles, making Adeline smile from the back seat of the car.

She was happy her sister had found a man like Jack who seemed to cherish the air he seemed to think she walked on. Cupid yipped from his seat beside her, his little seat harness holding him snug. He looked ridiculous but she reached over and petted his tiny head anyway. If anyone had small-man syndrome it was this dog. He was loud, obnoxious, and aggressive with anyone outside his pack. Lucky for her, he now considered her part of his pack.

They pulled into Jack's mother's home, and she unclipped Cupid and handed him off to Astrid. Jack grabbed the dessert she and Astrid had made early that morning—Hot cross bun bread and butter pudding. Apparently it was Jack's favourite and Astrid had wanted it perfect, so Adeline had agreed to help.

It had been a good distraction from the kiss she'd shared with Javier yesterday. Her cheeks heated as she remembered the way he'd taken her mouth and made her feel precious and desired yet still in control. A part of her was disappointed he'd pulled away, but a bigger part was relieved he'd had the sense to stop things before they went too far.

She'd been using her attraction to him to make herself feel good and to forget her problems and that was unfair to him. He was a good man, one who'd shown her nothing but kindness and patience. But she had to admit the attraction, despite what he'd thought, was real. She liked him—a lot and just acknowledging that made her feel guilty. How could she be falling for a guy when her baby was missing?

The front door swung open with a flourish and Jack's mother ushered them all inside. It was definitely cooler today, a stark difference from the sun of yesterday.

"Come in, come in. It's freezing out there."

Jack kissed his mother's cheek, as did Astrid, and Adeline stood there feeling awkward for half a second until she too was pulled into a warm hug. Surprised, she froze for a split second. The maternal hug, one so long denied her, brought an instant lump to her throat.

Carolyn Granger was the epitome of class, with cool blue eyes much like both her sons' and a sleek grey haircut that skimmed her shoulders, but her smile was open and welcoming as she pulled away and regarded Adeline.

"It's good to have you back, my dear. Welcome to the family."

Her words had the effect that her sister's words hadn't, for some reason this woman's easy acceptance and pleasure at seeing her made her relax.

Still holding on to Adeline, Carolyn turned to Jack. "Will and Aubrey are in the kitchen." She turned to Adeline, her eyes twinkling. "I put them to work on peeling the potatoes and carrots."

"Ma, what do you want done with this dessert?"

Carolyn let go and moved to Jack. "What do we have here?"

Jack told her and she grinned at Astrid. "Aren't I lucky to have two such wonderful daughters-in-law?"

"We aren't married yet, Ma."

Carolyn waved a hand. "Hooey. It's just semantics at this point."

"Carolyn, I'd love to take all the credit, but Addie did most of the work."

Adeline blushed as Carolyn looked at her with approval. "If only I had one more son."

"Ha, don't bother. I think Lopez has called dibs on her."

"Jack!" both women exclaimed at once.

He held up his hand that wasn't holding the dessert. "What? It's true and you know it." He turned to look at Astrid, and she softened instantly.

"Perhaps, but you can't call dibs on a woman, Jack. We're not objects."

"I know that, firefly, and I didn't mean it like that. I mean he likes her, and everyone knows it."

"Okay, I'm right here you know!" Addie waved and everyone went quiet. "Now, what can I do to help, Carolyn?"

"Can you make mint sauce?"

Adeline shrugged. "Never tried."

Carolyn took her hand and dragged her into the kitchen which was large and airy. "I'll teach you."

Will twisted from the sink and held up a potato and peeler in greeting. "Hey, Addie."

"Hi, Will. Good to see you, Aubrey."

Aubrey was slicing a savoy cabbage into ribbons as she too added a greeting.

The kitchen was the hub of this home and although Will and Jack didn't live there any longer she could see the familiar comfort as they joked and teased each other and their mother. As the day wore on and Carolyn shooed them out of her kitchen, they ended up in the lounge room or front room as Jack called it, because they had a lounge room in the front and one at the back.

Before they knew it, the conversation turned to wedding plans. Will and Aubrey had set a date for late autumn and Jack was eager to set a date for him and Astrid too.

"I can't set a date yet, Jack." Astrid dropped her eyes away and Adeline wondered at her sister's reticence. Was she unsure about her and Jack? She quickly dismissed that when she saw the love and affection between the two of them.

"Why not set a date, bee?"

Astrid smiled at her sister's nickname for her and leaned into Jack who wrapped his arm around her and kissed her cheek. "I want you to be my maid of honour and Payton to be one of the flower girls. It doesn't seem right to set a date until we have her home."

Adeline straightened her spine. "Set the date, Astrid. We'll be there one way or another."

Jack lifted his beer as he dragged Astrid onto his lap. "Damn straight."

After dinner, which consisted of the most tender leg of lamb she'd ever tasted with the mint sauce she'd made, they sat on the lounge as Jack and Will washed the dishes. She'd expected moaning or grumbling but was surprised when they'd stood and got stuck into the task.

"They're good boys, despite appearances."

"They're good men, Carolyn, and that's because of you," Astrid returned with a look toward the door.

Carolyn grinned, taking the compliment with grace. It was obvious how much she loved her family and Adeline felt honoured to be included in that, for today at least.

The doorbell rang and Carolyn looked over the couch toward the door. "I wonder who that could be."

"I'll get it, Ma," Jack called from the hallway.

Adeline listened intently, her heart kicking up when she heard the familiar deep voice of Javier. Sitting forward she tried not to look at the door but couldn't seem to help herself as she played with the hem of her cream, ballet-wrap jumper. She'd worn it to look nice for the public holiday Monday dinner with Jack's mother. Teamed with a pair of slim fitted trousers, for once she felt almost as glamourous as her sister.

"Hey, everyone. Addie."

She looked up at her name, heat slamming into her as she remembered the feel of those full soft lips commanding hers. His hair was wet, like he'd recently showered, and he was wearing dark jeans slung low on his hips and a tight white t-shirt that seemed to mould his body, outlining every muscle and sinew.

"Hey."

"Sorry to barge in but I need to talk to Jack about something and it's time sensitive."

Adeline stood, her mind on Payton and the urgency she could hear in his voice. "Is this about Payton?"

Lopez gave her a regretful look and shook his head, his hand reaching out for her and then dropping as if he'd suddenly remembered he shouldn't touch. But God, she wanted him to. She needed to feel his arms around her, to have him hold her together when she felt like splintering. She wasn't a weak woman who relied on others, especially men, but something about Javier made her feel safe enough to do that.

"It's not. I'm sorry."

Addie blinked rapidly and forced a smile she didn't feel. "Don't be, this isn't your fault." She turned to Astrid. "Where's the bathroom?" She needed a minute to compose herself and get herself under control again.

"Top of the stairs on the right."

Astrid went to stand and Addie stopped her, she needed a minute alone. "I'm fine."

Her sister gave her a tight smile. She'd been wonderful since the reunion and Adeline understood her hovering and worrying, she'd be the same, but Adeline was used to more alone time. As she closed the bathroom door and leaned against it, she took a shuddering breath and blew it out. She needed her baby home and this nightmare over. Moving to the toilet, she relieved her bladder and flushed before washing her hands and splashing her face with water.

She needed a place of her own. Maybe if Astrid saw her doing okay on her own, she wouldn't worry so much. She'd already put her family through enough, it was time to stand on her own two feet now she was feeling less like a newborn lamb.

Patting her face dry, she pinched her cheeks to get some colour back and opened the door. She gasped, her hand flying to her chest when she saw Javier leaning against the bannister at the top of the stairs.

He pushed off and walked toward her slowly. "You okay, Addie?"

He stopped just in front of her, and it took everything she had not to lean into his strength when he cupped her cheek with his big hand. His scent calmed her like nothing else could and she took courage from him. "I will be, I just need my baby home so I can plan the next step in my life." Her voice only wobbled a little.

"Aww, baby, we'll get her back, I promise." He hauled her into his arms and pressed his lips against her hair.

Her body melted into his and her arms wound around his waist as her face pressed against his chest. "Do you really believe that?"

He pulled away but kept her within the circle of his arms, his intense gaze on hers. "Yes, I do. I came here to update Jack. Hansen just passed through customs at Gatwick Airport."

Adeline's body went rigid and alert. "Joel Hansen?" That wasn't a coincidence and she told him so. "He's here for me."

"Let him come, he won't get far. Actually, it's saved us tracking the fucker down."

Adeline pulled from his arms knowing the longer she stayed the more natural it felt, and she needed to focus on her daughter. Javier let her go but she could see he didn't want to. "What's the plan now?"

Javier pushed his hand through his thick, dark hair and her fingers itched to do the same. Her hands balled into fists to stop the action and she stepped toward the stairs.

"Jack is calling the team in now for us to discuss a plan."

"Oh no, I'm ruining everyone's long weekend."

Javier smirked. "Babe, don't know if you noticed but we don't exactly work a nine to five job and for the record, I'm getting pissed at you taking the blame for all this when you're innocent."

Adeline didn't know what to say to that, so she remained silent.

He held his hand out for her to go first. "Shall we go make a plan?"

She nodded before stopping and turning to him. "Javier, thank you for everything. For helping, for sitting by my bedside, for being my friend."

He pursed his lips and lifted his chin. "It's not a chore to help someone you care about, Addie."

She frowned at that. "But you hardly knew me before this."

"Yeah, tell that to my brain. I feel like I've known you forever, like our souls are connected or something. Even if I didn't want to, there's no way I couldn't help. For the record, I want to."

He brushed his thumb over her bottom lip as he leaned toward her, so his body heat prickled her skin.

"Would you help me find a new place to stay?"

He cocked his head in surprise at her words. "You aren't happy with Jack and Astrid?"

"I am, but they're newly engaged, and I don't want to intrude."

"Yeah, I can imagine, and you have the Satan spawn dog."

"He's a little shit to be fair, but cute too."

"You know Jack and Astrid won't like this and will want you protected."

"I know, but if I get an alarm and make sure it's secure, then that would work."

"Actually, I may have a short-term idea. Let me make some calls, okay?"

"Okay." She smiled and it felt like the most genuine one since she'd woken from her nightmare and found her child really was gone.

CHAPTER NINE

It had taken everything in him to let her go and not kiss her, but she was vulnerable, and he was still keeping secrets. She didn't need more complications in her life and the two of them together, no matter how intense their chemistry was, was exactly that. Was offering her his spare room a mistake? Probably, but he couldn't stand the idea of her being anywhere else. At least in his home he had top-notch security and he could protect her.

He'd offer and see what she said. He knew exactly what Jack would say but he wasn't her keeper any more than he was his. He respected Jack as a boss and a friend, but Addie was different. Every moment they spent together he felt more and more like she was his, his what, he didn't know yet or maybe it was that he didn't want to acknowledge it.

Barking from the back of Eidolon drew his attention and he looked at the multiple screens to see Jack, Astrid, and Adeline walking toward the entrance. Rafe was already out the back of Eidolon with the dogs, running them through the assault course and doing training drills with them.

He'd wanted to bring Adeline with him but after their encounter on the stairs at Jack's mother's home, he didn't trust himself not to kiss her. He groaned, again thinking what a mistake it was to offer his spare room to her but knew he'd still do it.

"Hey, anyone else here yet?" Jack held the door for Astrid and Adeline who gave him a shy smile.

"Just Rafe."

Jack sat beside him and checked the monitors. "We should wait for the others to get here. Pax and Blake went to see his family and won't be back until tomorrow and Mitch and Autumn have both their families over so it might be tricky."

"Any word from Shadow?"

Lopez was intrigued by this new team. Jack was keeping the details close to the vest but what Lopez did know was that Jack knew what he was doing and if he thought they were warranted, then they absolutely were.

"Not yet. They'll only contact me when they have definitive intel. The day-to-day stuff will be handled internally."

Before Lopez could ask more, he saw Reid, Liam, Alex, and Gunner arrive, followed by Decker.

"Let's take this to the conference room. We have more space there."

Lopez grabbed his stuff and walked to the conference room, fighting the urge to check out Adeline's ass in those sexy as fuck fitted trousers. The others were joking amongst themselves, and he felt a twist of guilt in his belly at the secrets he was keeping. He needed to tell his friends the truth but first he owed it to Adeline.

He reached for her arm to stop her, and she turned to look at him with a question in her eyes. "Have you got a second before we go in?"

Adeline looked back at Astrid and nodded. "Sure."

Lopez pulled her into the kitchen which was empty and led her to a seat before letting her go and pulling his own chair closer as she put her hands between her knees.

"What's going on."

"We don't have much time, but I need to tell you something."

"Okaaaay." She drew the word out and he could hear she was beginning to get anxious.

"My father's name is Sandro Moura." He waited for a beat, watching for her reaction and the second it registered, her eyes widened, and she looked at him.

"Oh. My. God!" Her hand covered her lips, and she went to stand.

He stopped her. "Wait, Addie. I know you were the one who helped bring him down and you have no idea how grateful I am that you did."

Her skin paled even further. "How do you know that? I wasn't even working for the CIA then, not officially anyway."

"I know, you were a student and they recruited you when they realised your roommate was involved with Sandro."

She nodded. "Yes, Hansen recruited me and said if I helped, I'd be getting a dangerous man off the streets. I had no idea until after it was over who he was or what he'd done, or I never would've agreed."

"They offered to pay all your student debt and give you the gig as a scientist with the medical program."

"Yes, it was way better funded than any other and it had the capacity to do so much good. Or it would've had it been real. After he was arrested, they followed through on their word and I thought I was done but as I later learned, I was an asset to them and they essentially owned me." Her eyes were clear as she straightened her spine and folded her arms in a defensive move, and he hated that she was closing herself off to him. "So, all this has been to find out, what? Why I did it or to get revenge for putting him in jail?"

Lopez shook his head, and he gripped her upper arm. "God no, at least not all of it. I'm glad he's in prison. He ruined my mother's life, and mine. His being put away was the best feeling ever but I do have questions only you can answer."

Addie cocked her head. Her eyes were cool now, and he hated that. "So, you want what? Answers?"

Lopez swallowed and knew honesty was the only answer here,

even though he could see her walls coming up and her emotions close off. "Yes." He always found it hard to talk about this next bit and avoided doing so as much as possible. He found keeping to the facts was the best way to stop the barrel load of emotion and guilt from burying him alive. "He killed my mother and I have no idea where he buried her body. I want to bring her home and give her the burial she deserves."

"Oh, Javier, I'm so sorry." Her eyes went soft, and he saw the pity in them.

Shaking his head, he caressed her cheek with his thumb. "It's okay. Well, no, it isn't, and it never will be, but I've learned to live with it. My father is an evil man and I just want this last piece of the puzzle so I can close the door."

"And you think I have it."

"You're the only person alive that spent any time with him outside of the cartel. He may have told you something that you don't realise is important."

Addie bit her lip and he wanted to soothe the pink flesh with his tongue. "I can't think of anything right now but when this is over, I'll help you if I can."

"You will?"

She smiled and nodded her head. "Yes. I won't say that I'm happy you lied to me or made me believe we had something more to get what you needed but I do understand. There's nothing I wouldn't do to protect Payton and I can see you loved your mother very much."

"She was all I had growing up." He scooted forward so he could take her hand and convey his message so that she truly understood him. "I never lied to you, Addie. I care about you very much, way more than I wanted to or planned. Every single encounter we've shared has been real. Yes, I kept something from you, and I was wrong but not even Jack knows about our connection. The only person who worked it out is Decker."

"Even so, it feels like a lie, and I have enough going on without having to try and second guess how I feel about you or our every conversation. I like you, Javier, but I think for now we should be friends. I have to concentrate on Payton."

"And after, when she's home and settled?"

"Then we can see what happens, but my life is a mess. I have no job, no home, and the fricking CIA and God only knows who else, want me dead."

"You're not a mess, Addie, you're a warrior and a damn sexy one." He grinned when she squinted at him. "But I'll agree to just being friends if you'll let me help you with your housing issue."

"Tell me more."

He saw the twinkle light her eyes and smiled in return. "I have a spare room. Come and stay with me. Just as friends, of course. I can't cook but I promise there'll be zero romantic action going on to nauseate you."

Addie laughed as he'd intended. "They are nauseatingly in love."

"Right?"

"Okay, but I have to pay rent or help out. I can't keep being everyone's charity case."

"Do you cook?"

"Pretty well."

"How about you cook in exchange for a room?"

"Fine and I'll try and remember anything I can about your father."

Lopez blinked, having almost forgotten this was what had started this whole thing for him. Somehow the truth of his past was becoming less important than his present and future. "Thank you. Now I need to go and tell my team what I've kept from them."

"You don't have to on my account."

He stood and offered her his hand, which she took, letting him pull her to standing. Her body was so close he could almost touch her when he inhaled, her breasts centimetres from his chest. This was going to be an exercise in restraint of epic proportions. "I do. We've kept secrets in this team before and it almost ripped us apart. I won't do that to them again."

Addie smiled. "Alrighty then. We better go before they send out a search party."

Lopez held the door and followed her out and into the conference room. He could hear chatting as he pushed open the door and all eyes moved to him and Addie.

Jack eyed him warily. "About damn time."

"Sorry. I needed a quick word with Addie."

"Everything okay?"

"Yes, but I need to tell you all something."

Lopez looked around the room and caught the look of approval from Decker, who was standing near the back in biker leathers instead of his usual suit. He must have been out on his bike when he got the call from Jack. Decker was the least biker looking of them all, but he frequently went out on his Ducati. Lopez thought it was his way of trying to outrun his pain as he was always more likely to go out on holidays or family times.

Lopez took a deep breath and proceeded to tell his team and friends about his past and his connection to Adeline. He noted the tension in Jack's shoulders and the surprise on Astrid's face that turned to a frown as she imagined his desire to be close to Addie as nefarious. The rest of the men, including Rafe who he didn't know well, had impassive looks on their faces, showing no emotion whatsoever.

It was more than a little unnerving to face this group. Even knowing they were his allies they were still a very formidable bunch. He'd rather the anger of a pissed off glare than the poker faces he faced.

Liam was leaning back in his chair, his leg crossed over his knee and his hands behind his head. "Any reason you kept this from us all?"

"I knew some of it." Decker leaned forward and shot Lopez a look of support. "The rest I worked out."

"I knew, too."

Jack's words shocked him, and Lopez felt his eyes bug. "You did?"

Jack looped his fingers and leaned his forearms on the table as he lifted his chin at Decker. "Same as Deck. I obviously knew about your father as that's in your file, but I worked the rest out when you showed an interest in Adeline. You're my friend, Lopez, but she's my family and I had to make sure she was safe above all else."

Lopez glanced at her to see her reaction, but she was looking at Jack and Astrid.

"Why didn't you say anything?"

Lopez was amazed Jack had held back from confronting him and wondered if it had anything to do with the woman who even now had her hand on his shoulder as if trying to calm him.

"Astrid trusted you not to be a dick and I trust her. But not only that, I know you, Lopez, and you're a valued member of this team. I trusted you to do the right thing and you have." Jack lifted his hand and pointed a finger at him as he frowned. "But let me say this. If you hurt her, I'll cut your balls off and feed them to Cupid for breakfast."

Lopez felt the wince from several of the others and saw Mitch shift in his seat at the images Jack's words evoked.

Adeline held her hands up, palm to the ceiling, eyebrows raised. "Do I get any say in this at all?"

"Of course! Which testicle would you like me to cut off first?"

Adeline snorted at Jack's question and the wink he threw her, and she shook her head.

"Anyway, we're getting off track. Tell me what you know about Hansen. If you lot have issues, take it up with Lopez after the meeting."

Lopez glanced around the room as the others shrugged as if accepting that if Jack knew and was okay with it, then they were too. It was why he considered this group family above all else. They had your back in good times and bad and if you fucked up, forgiveness was given— eventually.

"Joel Hansen passed through customs at Gatwick Airport at ten-thirty this morning. He had another man with him, who I've identi-fied as Jacob Einhorn." Lopez hit the button on this monitor and the image of the two men filled the screen. He couldn't help looking at Adeline to see her reaction and was relieved to see her calm and focused.

"Hansen and Einhorn are known associates from years back, the two met at college. Einhorn now works at Quantico as an instructor, so it's strange he's travelling with him as the two agencies aren't known for playing nice together. I'm going to run an in-depth background on Einhorn and see what pops."

"Do you think he's here for me?"

Adeline sat ramrod straight with her shoulders back and her head up. She was poised and dignified but he could see the fear and anger she was trying to control.

He was about to answer when Reid shot to his feet. "We're about to find out."

Lopez's eyes shot to the monitors on the other side of the room, and he saw Hansen and Einhorn at the main gate. The atmosphere in the room became charged, as if every neuron in every person was electrified and ready for a fight.

"Motherfucker is dead."

Jack charged from the room and Astrid shot after him.

"Jack, you need to be cool," Decker warned as they all followed behind.

Lopez took position behind Adeline, wanting to be close to her as Gunner and Waggs closed in on either side of her.

At the main door Jack stopped and radioed the gate to tell them to let Hansen and Einhorn through.

"Search them," Jack demanded of Reid and Liam as the two men stepped outside while Mitch covered them.

Hansen looked calm and in control, his hands out in surrender while Einhorn looked uncomfortable and seemed to be trying not to show it. Hansen was tall with medium brown hair, a clean-shaven jaw, and a slim build. He was good looking Lopez supposed but the fact he used that to lure women into becoming pawns in his power games made him ugly as fuck.

"This is unnecessary. Just give us Adeline and we'll be on our way."

Lopez fists clenched at his sides in an effort to hold himself back.

Reid and Liam nodded at Jack, giving the men the all-clear and Jack opened the door and stepped out, putting himself between Hansen and Astrid. Lopez moved in front of Adeline to block the asshole from getting anywhere near her. His desire to protect her from this man who'd hurt her in so many ways was almost physical. His brain was screaming at him that she was his. His to protect and his to love. The sudden thought coming at such an odd time made him pause before he shoved it away. Now wasn't the time to start considering his feelings.

Jack got in his face, poking his pointer finger in the man's chest. "Have you been smoking crack? Because if you think I'm letting you anywhere near Adeline or Astrid, you're fucking high."

Lopez could feel the Baltic fury that was running through Jack's veins, and it was terrifying.

"She's a CIA asset and is wanted in connection with murder charges."

Lopez felt her hand on his back as her fingers curled into his shirt. He wanted to reassure her but didn't want to take his eyes off Hansen or Einhorn.

"You have no jurisdiction here and even if you did, she's under the protection of the Crown."

Hansen went red and his lip twitched in anger as he tried to look at Adeline over Lopez's shoulder.

"Don't fucking look at her," Lopez spat, his temper beginning to fray.

Hansen looked him over with a condescending glare. "And who are you?"

Lopez folded his arms as he felt his brothers in all but name move closer to him and Adeline and Astrid. "Your worst fucking nightmare if you come near Adeline or Astrid again."

Lopez wasn't a man to make threats, and when he did his team knew they weren't empty.

Hansen and Einhorn, who hadn't said a word but seemed to be back-up of some sort, stepped back. He looked at Jack, then Astrid, before his attention came back to him and Addie.

"This isn't over." Hansen pointed. "This isn't over."

Jack moved forward a foot to follow him, but Astrid grabbed his biceps. Jack glanced back at the woman he loved before turning his cold gaze on Hansen and Einhorn. "Damn right it isn't. But fair warning, if you step foot on my property or within a thousand feet of Astrid or Adeline ever again, you'll be fed through a straw for the rest of your miserable life."

"Do the right thing, Adeline," Hansen called as he opened his car door.

Lopez lost his calm, a growl erupting from his throat as he rushed to get to Hansen. He'd never wanted to kill someone as badly as he did Hansen. He felt arms around his chest and saw Mitch appear in front of him as he struggled to get out of Alex's hold.

"Cool it. Don't let him win."

Lopez shrugged and stopped fighting. "I'm good, let me go."

He turned and headed back inside while Liam closed and locked the door behind them.

He felt Adeline beside him as they headed back to the conference room. "Are you okay?"

Her hand was light on his arm, but he felt the electricity from her touch shoot over his skin. He linked his fingers with hers and stopped outside the door to the room where everyone else was now waiting, including a ranting Jack.

"Me? Of course." He rubbed his other hand over her arm and up her shoulder to cup the back of her neck. "Are you okay?"

Adeline tilted her head toward his touch as his thumb worked over the delicate skin. "I can't believe I ever fell for that piece of shit."

Lopez grinned at her words and her spirit. "He is kind of a

douche bag. What were you thinking?" His attempt to lighten the mood worked and she laughed.

"I have no clue, but rest assured I'm cured. I like my men with a side of geek. Muscles and brains are my new kryptonite."

Lopez felt his blood heat with desire for this woman, not just because he wanted to be inside her and feel her beneath him, but because he wanted her heart. "I have a confession."

His thumb rubbed over her bottom lip and her eyes went dark with desire as her breathing quickened. "Oh? What is it?"

"I don't think I'll be able to keep my hands off you if you move into my spare room."

"Oh!"

He felt disappointment like lead in his gut when she pulled away, the feel of her curves gone from his arms. "Where are you going?"

Adeline turned and offered him a secret smile. "To pack."

CHAPTER TEN

ADELINE SHOVED the rest of her meagre possessions into a holdall and zipped it closed as her sister sat on the bed, cuddling the demon dog.

"Are you sure this is the right thing to do?"

Astrid and Jack had been unsure of her plan to move in with Javier as his roommate. Jack worried she wouldn't be protected and she knew Astrid worried because her sister saw the attraction between them and wanted to protect her heart.

Adeline sighed and sat on the bed beside Astrid. "Yes. You and Jack are newly engaged and the last thing you need is to have a third wheel thrown into the mix."

Astrid pouted. "You are not a third wheel. You're my sister and I love you."

"I know you do, and I love you too. You've always watched out for me, Astrid. Even though you were the youngest you were always the most protective and street smart."

"Yeah, well I didn't have that big, old brain of yours, so I had to have something."

"Are you kidding me? I was always envious of you, the way boys looked at you as if you hung the moon. You're fire and grit. The fight and energy you put into protecting others made you my hero."

Astrid wiped a tear from her cheek. "You were mine, Addie."

Adeline leaned in and hugged her sister, avoiding Cupid who tolerated her more than most. "This is the best for both of us. You need time with Jack, and I need to feel strong again and part of that is standing on my own two feet."

Astrid sniffed. "Are you sure it's not about the sexy geek who can't keep his eyes or hands off you?"

Adeline grinned. "Maybe that's part of it. Javier makes me feel strong and protected at the same time."

Astrid nodded. "I get it, Jack does the same for me. He makes me feel like I can conquer the world, but he's there to catch me and break my fall if I fail."

"Well, this is one mission I can't fail. I have to get Payton back. She must be so scared."

"If she's anything like you, she'll be fine."

"Actually, she reminds me a lot of you. I can't wait for you to meet her."

"Me neither. Eidolon will get her back. Jack says Shadow already has someone inside the Ravelino mansion."

Adeline stood and walked to her bathroom to grab her toiletries and pack them. She couldn't think about Payton too much. She'd had to shut her emotions off for fear she'd completely break down and be of no use to her daughter if she did.

"Do you think he's keeping her in the main house?" Adeline woke in the night wondering if her child was cold or scared or if they were treating her okay.

"Definitely inside the house. Especially if he believes she's his daughter. He'll want her close. Maybe even get to know her."

Adeline shivered at the thought of that monster being anywhere near Payton but if he believed she was his daughter, it would keep her safe. He might be a monster, but he considered himself a family man and children were off-limits.

"Has Iago said anything?"

Adeline had been told by Jack that Iago was a prisoner in the United Kingdom and had been tried and convicted over an attempt on the Queen. He and his men had all been found guilty and were serving life sentences.

"No, not yet, but Jack and Alex have a plan."

"What is it?"

"There are certain rules here. Eidolon needs to get him alone so they can interview him without eyes on them. Plus, they have two men watching Hansen and Einhorn around the clock. That man can't fart without Eidolon knowing thanks to Lopez and Gunner."

Adeline wrinkled her nose. "I can't believe we both fell for his bullshit."

Astrid put her finger in her mouth and motioned gagging. "I claim temporary insanity."

"Ha, me too but at least you didn't get knocked up by him."

"True, you win idiot of the year on that one."

Adeline laughed. "I don't regret a single thing because it gave me my child, who is my world." Tears sprang from the laughter, and she blinked them back trying to get a handle on things.

"Hey."

Astrid stood and plopped Cupid on the floor, who ran to look for Jack downstairs. Astrid put her arms around her, and Adeline breathed in her sister's perfume.

"We'll get her back and then we're going to go dress shopping for the most awesome flower girl dress we can find."

Addie sniffed and wiped a tear from her cheek. "Absolutely."

A horn outside beeped and Addie felt her heart kick in her chest at the thought of moving into Javier's spare room after what he'd said and what she'd intimated to him. She wasn't sure if she should want this, but she was sure she did.

Astrid lifted her bag and carried it down the stairs for her. Jack was waiting at the bottom and moved toward her, opening his arms.

Adeline went into them, instantly enveloped in a warm hug that felt safe, like a big brother's would.

"If you need us, call day or night. And if you can't stand living with Lopez you always have a bed here."

"I'm only going down the road, Jack, but thank you. You hardly know me, but you've put everything on hold to help me get Payton back and I'll never be able to repay that."

Jack's eyes twinkled. "You already did. You looked out for the woman I love when you were growing up."

"I failed in the end though."

Jack shook his head. "No, you didn't. Look at her, she's magnificent."

Adeline looked at her sister who was blinking away tears. "She is pretty awesome and I'm glad she found you."

"She was a persistent pain in my ass until I couldn't ignore her."

Addie laughed. "Yep, that sounds like her."

"Hey!" Astrid frowned in mock indignation and laughed.

Adeline pulled out of Jack's arms, and he immediately reached for Astrid. That was what she wanted—a man who couldn't go more than ten minutes without wanting to hold her or touch her. A man who looked at her as if she held the secrets of the universe in her hand, the way Jack did Astrid. Not just a man who followed her like a puppy but one who could challenge her and make her body burn with desire and need. A man like Javier. Regardless of his secrets and his ill-conceived plan to find out his father's secrets, he was a good man.

She would know, she'd had more than her share of bad ones. It was hard to conceive that he was Sandro's son until she'd looked closer and could see the similarities in the jaw line and the eyes but where Sandro had been cold, Javier was warm and kind. But both were incredibly smart, and she knew she had to keep her guard up. If she found out Javier wasn't the man she thought he was, she'd be devastated. She had to protect herself against that while she explored the possibility of them having something.

Javier was coming up the front path when Jack opened the door and grinned a cheeky, sexy smile that made her belly flip. "You ready?"

He reached for her bag, and she let him take it as she hugged Astrid. "Call me later if you want and if not, I'll see you in the morning at Eidolon."

"Sure, love you."

"Love you, baby sis."

Javier opened the car door and she got in, her hand moving over the soft leather of the Mercedes E-class. "Nice ride."

"Yeah, I love it."

They chatted about menial stuff as he drove, and it felt more important than just her moving into his spare room. This felt like a life-changing event in some ways which was silly. Whatever they were was temporary, no matter how much chemistry they had. When she got Payton back, she'd need to focus all her attention on her child. She'd need to find her feet and a job, make sure her daughter was okay, and throwing a man into her life just wasn't an option.

Javier opened the door of his home which was a detached two-storey with wood cladding and white masonry on the front. He led her into a spacious hallway with wood flooring, a door to the left led into a large lounge and on the right an open plan kitchen diner.

"Wow. This is beautiful."

He quirked a brow at her. "I'd like to say this was all me, but the truth is, I bought the show home already decorated because I'm useless with this kind of thing. Let me show you your room and then we can decide on dinner." Javier moved up the stairs with her bags and led her past two doors on the left.

"That's my room, then you have the home office, bathroom, and on the right is your room. It doesn't have an en-suite but mine does, so you have it to yourself anyway."

The room had cream carpet, a king-sized bed with champagne coloured bedding, and pale pink walls that looked almost white.

"The wardrobe is clear, and you have a TV there." He stepped toward the shutters which were closed and pulled them open to reveal a delightful Juliette balcony.

Adeline stepped forward. "Oh wow, what a view."

She felt Javier move beside her, the air around them stilling as she looked at the view of the mountains through the glass. "It's so beautiful."

"It is."

She turned at the rasp in his voice to find his eyes on her and her breath caught in her chest. He was so handsome, with his wavy hair that didn't seem to want to sit how he wanted and kept flopping forward no matter how many times he pushed it back. The flex of his biceps and the hard muscles she knew were hidden beneath his shirt made her fingers itch to touch him. She wanted to feel his lips on hers, especially as she knew he kissed her like the rest of the world didn't exist.

He shook his head and stepped back, and she sighed.

"I'll leave you to get settled. Come down when you're ready and we can sort out what we'll do for dinner."

"I thought cooking was my department instead of rent?"

"Not tonight. We can order take-out and you can relax for a bit."

He winked and her insides went liquid. No other man had ever had this effect on her, and she wished they'd met under different circumstances. Adeline unpacked her meagre things and hung them in the wardrobe. She checked out the bathroom and placed her brush and shampoo in the cupboard.

As she came out, she saw his bedroom door was open. Unable to resist, she poked her head in and the scent of his cologne hit her like a wall of sexual seduction. His room was exactly like she'd imagined. A navy-blue quilt cover, cream deep-pile carpet, white walls, blue drapes, an enormous television on the wall, and dark wood wardrobe and drawers. A quirky industrial style lamp sat on the unit by his bed on what she assumed was his side, with a pair of glasses she recognised as his and an open book lay face down.

Curious, she moved closer to see what he was reading, wanting to know everything about this man. She almost tripped over a dumbbell on the floor and narrowly missed swearing and alerting the man below that she was snooping around his room.

She picked up the book, careful not to lose his place and read the cover, her eyes going wide, her lips tipping into a smile. Javier Lopez was reading Me Before You by JoJo Moyes.

"Watcha doin'?"

Adeline screeched, dropping the book as she jumped in fright at the sound of Javier's voice right behind her. Her hand flew to her chest, and she leaned forward to catch her breath and calm her racing heart. "Jesus, you made me jump."

Javier bent to pick up the book and glanced at her as he placed it on his bedside table face down once more.

"I was just... um...."

"Being nosey?" He pursed his lips, and she could see he was trying hard not to laugh.

Adeline folded her arms and huffed. "Yes, fine. I was being nosey."

Javier laughed and pulled her closer to his body, his hands on her hips. "It's fine. You know all my secrets now, even the fact I read women's fiction."

Addie eyed the book to try and distract herself from the effect he had on her, especially in his room next to his bed, surrounded by his scent.

"Yeah, that was a bigger shock than your dad actually."

Javier ducked his head to catch her gaze, and his was liquid desire. "It's Evelyn's."

A wave of jealousy swam through her at the thought of him with another woman. She shut it down feeling foolish because anyone who saw Alex and Evelyn together knew they were the kind of soulmates that poets wrote about. "Oh."

"She left it in the kitchen at work and I picked it up thinking it was something else. I started reading and wanted to know how it ends."

"You're such a contradiction, Javier Lopez. You're sweet and kind and funny, but you also have a protective alpha streak a mile wide. I can't figure you out."

"I'm just me."

He shrugged as if he didn't know what to tell her and she realised he didn't see how awesome he was. He was the whole package and was totally unaware of it—clever, gorgeous, and had a body that would make models weep. He was an alpha with just the right amount of sweet and he was hard to resist.

"Well, I for one think you're amazing. You've helped me more than you know."

His thumb was rubbing light circles on her hip, and she felt the pulse of desire between her legs, her nipples tightened, and she wanted him to kiss her so badly it hurt.

He pulled away and she almost swayed it was so sudden. "So, what do you fancy for dinner?"

"Um, don't mind."

She followed him down the stairs trying not to watch the way the denim stretched over his sexy butt. They reached the kitchen, and he took out his phone as he leaned on the other side of the counter facing her.

"Okay, we have, Chinese, Indian, Thai, pizza, Italian, or there's a place that just does desserts."

"What do you want?"

Javier raised a brow. "Something you'll learn about me, Addie, is that I'll literally eat anything. I'm the human equivalent of a trash can."

Addie wrinkled her nose. "Gross."

Javier shrugged one shoulder. "Meh, I think I went hungry one too many times to take any kind of food for granted."

Guilt and sadness assailed her at the thought of a little Javier hungry. "I'm sorry."

"Don't be. I had what mattered and I had enough. My mother made everything seem like an adventure, even the hard times."

"You miss her."

"Every day."

Adeline loved how honest he was about his love for his mother and how he spoke of her with a smile even though she could see it hurt him still. "Will you tell me about her?"

"Yes, but can we order food first? I'm starving."

"Yes, and Chinese sounds good." She moved to stand closer to him so she could see over his shoulder what was on the menu. He turned and his lips were so close she could almost feel the tingle she knew they'd cause. "Get me shrimp chow mein please."

"Sure." He finished placing the order and placed his phone on the counter. "It'll be about forty-five minutes." He went to the fridge and held up a bottle of pinot. "Glass of wine?"

She nodded. Javier poured them both a glass and slid hers across the counter.

"So, Jack told me all the Eidolon homes are on a security loop and you can increase the level of security and put yourselves on a higher alert if needed."

Javier took a sip of his wine. "Yeah, Will built it. Basically, we all have top-notch security because of what we do but we can level that up if we feel we're under threat. So, for instance, with you here this place is levelled up. The exterior will be watched 24/7 by one of the team and the doors and windows are reinforced. There's a boat load of other stuff which will bore you to tears, but you can sleep at night knowing you're as safe as houses."

"That's good to know." It felt shameful to her that she was happy to be safe when her child was with strangers and probably scared and confused. It had been months now and every part of her wanted to get on a flight to the Ravelino mansion and march up to the gate to demand her back. She knew they'd kill her though, so she had to be clever and allowing Shadow to find her and do recon without the cartel knowing was best.

"Hey, where did you go?"

Adeline blinked to see Javier in front of her and shook off her maudlin thoughts. "Just thinking about Payton."

"Addie." He cupped her cheek, stroking her with his thumb. "I can't imagine how hard this is for you."

"It's torture. I try not to think about it and then feel guilty for that. I just want her back."

"We'll get her back, I promise you."

Adeline looked into his dark eyes and believed every word he was saying, she had to, or she'd fall apart.

Their food arrived and broke the tense sadness. Javier plated it up and they ate at the counter.

"So, tell me about your mother."

Javier scooped a piece of lemon chicken into his mouth and chewed. "She was barely five feet tall and had long black hair that she always wore in a ponytail down her back. She was an amazing cook and could make even the blandest food taste wonderful. She was a seamstress and made wedding dresses. Her family were rich, they made their money in banking. When she fell in love with my father, who was a poor kid from the favela, they disowned her. She and my father married and had me. From what she said they were happy for a while and then he lost his job at a local garage and things began to go wrong. He turned to the cartels for help, and they gave him jobs that became more and more dangerous. She begged him not to do them, but he was lost by then and my mother left. Took me across the country and we never saw him again."

"Wow, that's so sad. Did your mom's family help her out?"

"Nope, they told her she'd made her bed and shamed them and now she had to lie in it. My mother gave me everything. We had a tiny apartment, but it was clean, and I was loved, and she worked her fingers to the bone to make sure I had everything she could give me. I was happy."

Adeline pushed her half-eaten plate of food away. "Do you remember your father?"

"Bits and pieces, more of a feeling than anything tangible. I know my mother loved him up until the day she died and wouldn't hear a thing against him. She said I didn't know him like she did. Even after he got the reputation he did, she wouldn't hear a bad word. It was the only time we fought."

"What makes you think he killed her?"

"He was the last person to see her before she vanished. I know if she was alive, she'd have found a way to let me know."

Adeline placed a hand over his, offering comfort because she wasn't sure she could give him anything else. "I didn't know him well. We only spoke a few times. My job was to make sure that anything he did say was recorded. He never said a word though and they only caught him because from there, they managed to follow him and catch him in the act. He flipped after that. I always thought he admitted everything too quickly. It was almost as if he wanted to be caught because he knew it was his only way out. He never turned on Ravelino though, although it was leaked that he had."

"It's funny, I hate him for what he did and how he broke my mother's heart, yet I still find myself curious."

"That's normal. You share DNA. It's natural to be curious about him. Have you thought of visiting and asking him outright?"

Javier shook his head. "No. I just don't know if I could do it."

Adeline smothered a yawn. "Sorry."

"It's fine. It's been a hell of a day. You should get some sleep. The next few days could be busy chasing up leads."

"I hope so, I really want my girl home."

Javier moved, taking the plates to the sink and rinsed them before putting them in the dishwasher.

That night as she lay in bed thinking of her daughter and Javier and how his childhood had affected him and how he'd turned out pretty well adjusted. He was a good man despite his father's abandonment and the shadow he cast over his life. Was she a fool to hope for the same for Payton, that this period of her life wouldn't leave scars?

She wished Javier would quit being a gentleman and make love to her or fuck her brains out so she could shut her brain off for just a bit.

CHAPTER ELEVEN

"Here, drink this. It might stop you from being such grumpy guts." Alex set a coffee down on Lopez's desk and sat in a nearby chair.

Lopez wasn't in the mood for company, he was tired, having spent half the night fantasising about Adeline naked in the room across from him. He didn't even know if she slept naked, but his brain didn't seem to give a shit. "Thanks." He took a sip and winced as it burned his tongue, but it was worth it for the liquid nirvana that flooded his system.

"So, what's up with you anyway?"

"Nothing, just tired."

"Fucking tell me about it. I spend every night on edge waiting for Evelyn to tell me it's time and flinching at every movement or sound she makes. Then when I do fall asleep, she needs to pee because our child is using her bladder like a trampoline apparently, and I jump as if I just got shot."

"Gee, Alex, you make parenthood sound so appealing."

Alex grinned. "I can't wait. It's like Christmas and birthdays all thrown into one with a side of Halloween for the abject terror I feel that I might fuck this up."

Lopez shook his head, happy to have his mind off Adeline and how to help her get her daughter back. "Nah, you'll be an amazing father. Out of all of us you're the most natural after Waggs and Mitch."

Alex brushed his hands through his hair. "I hope you're right. So, tell me what you're working on—distract me."

Lopez sat forward and moved his mouse to wake his screen. "I've been looking into Hansen and Einhorn. Hansen is up to his neck in something. He has two offshore bank accounts under shell corps. One has two million in it and the other has been receiving a million a month for the last six months and now has six million in it."

Alex whistled. "Wow, that's a lot of hidden secrets."

"Yeah, my thoughts exactly. I've asked Will to hack the CIA files again as he's slicker than me and less likely to get caught. I want to know more about one file called Operation Cradle. It's the same time-line from when Adeline went undercover with Ravelino. I've done some digging and it looks like around that time there was an investigation into pregnant women going missing. Hansen was heading up the case and just like that it was shut down, and no mention is made of it again."

Alex sat forward and Lopez wondered if this was the wrong thing to share with a man who was about to have a child. "Not even police reports?"

"Nothing, they're all gone. I've searched everywhere."

"Does Jack know about this?"

"I was just about to tell him, but he's out walking that damned dog of his."

Alex smirked. "He is a total melt over that dog. If I hadn't seen it with my own eyes, I'd never believe it."

"I know, right."

Alex pointed back at the screen. "Back to this for a second. Is it in any way linked to Ravelino?"

"I can't find evidence of that, but my gut says yes. The way Hansen put both Adeline and Astrid undercover, slept with them both, and especially the way he left them to die when they needed an extract. This guy is dirty as fuck. I just need proof."

"Then let's find it. What can I do?"

Lopez felt relief that he was getting some help and he knew it was taking Alex's mind off Evelyn. His own mind began to wander, and he tried to imagine what a child of his would look like and all he could see was a little girl who looked like Adeline, not Payton because he'd seen her picture and she was beautiful, all smiles and blonde hair like her aunt. No, this little girl looked like Addie and him. The thought shocked him, and he wondered if it was a lack of blood to his brain.

He'd spent all last night lying in bed wishing he'd taken her up on her silent invitation. He'd known he could've had her in his bed. He wasn't being an arrogant prick, it was the truth, he'd seen it in her eyes, felt it in the hitch of her breath. She wanted him but he'd held back not wanting to rush her or take advantage and he still felt the tiniest bit of reservation from her, as if she was ashamed for wanting him.

He knew it had nothing to do with him, or at least he hoped to God it didn't, but it was more about her allowing herself to feel good when her child was missing. He'd missed her at breakfast, having deliberately made himself scarce when Astrid picked her up to take her somewhere.

The door opened and Jack poked his head in. "Conference room, now. We have eyes on Payton."

Lopez scrambled to his feet and followed Alex and Jack out the door. His senses were heightened by a flash of adrenalin in his blood. Finally, they had eyes on the child. He looked for Adeline when he went in and took his usual seat, but she was nowhere to be seen and neither was Astrid.

Seeing him looking around Jack answered his unspoken question. "I called and they're on their way."

Mitch, Gunner, and Waggs came in still wearing gym clothes and covered in sweat. Liam and Decker wore their usual, jeans and a t-shirt for Liam, and a suit for Decker. Rafe came in last with Ziggy, the Malinois, beside him. He sat at the end and the dog sat beside him and lay down at his hand command.

"I'm not going to wait for Adeline and Astrid as time is of the essence. I had word from Bás that his man Bein has eyes on Payton. He confirmed it's her and she's being held inside the main house. As far as Bein can tell she's being cared for and seems to be mainly looked after by a nanny."

Jack pressed a button, and a grainy image came on screen of a blonde child, which was no doubt Payton, in the gardens of the Ravelino mansion.

"As we know, the Ravelino cartel are slippery as fuck and Juan managed to get out of his conviction after only two years in jail. Lopez believes Hansen is in league with Juan in some way and I'm inclined to agree. Hansen let both our girls rot but he didn't give them up until after they wanted an extract, which says Hansen is after something too. We need to get in and get Payton out, but that place is a fucking fortress since Adeline and Astrid escaped him. Bein and Duchess report multiple canines and up to thirty guards. There's an electric fence, and the guards are armed to the teeth with semi-automatics. I say we meet up with Bás, Bein, and Duchess and form a plan."

"I know Bás, but who are the others, Jack? Do we trust them?" Liam asked the question, his arms folded over his chest and Lopez remembered that not everyone was aware of Shadow.

"They're part of the new team I founded that, until now, were unknown to anyone here. Now, it's clear that everyone at Eidolon needs to be aware of their existence. But their identities don't, even under the pain of death, leave this room. If we're ghosts, then they're ghosts of ghosts if that's even a fucking thing."

"Roger that. Was everyone in the dark?" Liam seemed a little miffed.

"No, it was a need to know, and some team members needed to

know but I should've told you all. I'll make the necessary introductions on the flight over by video call. Will set it up so it's secure "

Liam seemed fine with that, and Lopez's shoulders relaxed. He hated when the team had any angst, the last two years had seen enough of that, and it was finally in a place where everyone was cool again.

"Alex, you and Blake hold down the fort here. If anything happens with Evelyn, Blake can step up." Alex nodded his agreement. "The rest of us are wheels up in four hours. Go home, pack a bag, and meet at the airfield in three hours. We can form a plan on the flight. Lopez, bring all the tech you can. Liam, make sure the jet is fully loaded with our gear."

The men began to file out and he waited for Jack so he could update him on what he'd found out about Hansen.

"Fucker is dirty. I can't wait to bury him in his own shit."

"You and me both, boss man."

Jack eyed him over his crossed arms as he leaned on the desk. "How's Adeline?"

"As well as can be expected. She's obviously worried, but I made sure she ate and got some sleep and I think being out of the house helps her to feel less of a burden."

"That was never our intention. Astrid adores her sister and just wants what's best for her."

Lopez palmed the back of his neck. "She knows that, and she's grateful, but I think she feels a little lost at sea, like the sand keeps shifting beneath her feet and she wanted to take control of her life. Choosing where to sleep is one of those things she can do. Plus, I think she feels like she's messing things up for a newly engaged couple."

"I get that, but as long as she isn't angry with Astrid."

Lopez chuckled. "So protective of her."

"Damn right, and when it happens to you, we'll talk again. Or maybe it already has?"

"Don't book the church yet, Jack. Adeline and I are friends."

"But you like her?"

"Jesus, Jack, what is this? Have our cycles synced?"

"Fuck off, Lopez. I just care about her because she's family now and I could think of worse men for her to end up with. Plus, if you start dating, she might decide to stay here and that makes my firefly happy."

"I think there was a compliment in there somewhere."

"Yeah maybe, but don't get too excited, you're still not good enough for her. Are you going to wait for Adeline and drive her home to pack?"

"Yeah, I'll be in the tech room."

"I'll send her in as soon as they arrive and I've updated them. I'd prefer they stay here but there's no chance of that so...." Jack shrugged in a what can you do gesture.

Lopez went to start packing his stuff up, at least the equipment he knew the team would need the most. He'd done this a thousand times and his mind wandered as he completed his task. Jack was right, he wasn't good enough. He had a shitty father, had come from nothing, and had lied to her but he couldn't help that feeling of completeness when he was around her. It wasn't just the fact he wanted to bury himself inside her and stay there for days, or taste the sweetness of her skin, hear her beg and scream his name as she came, it was more.

She was sweet, and kind, resilient too and he found himself telling her things he'd never shared with anyone else. Just last night he'd shared more about his mother than he ever had, telling Adeline about her dressmaking and her relationship with his father.

"Hey, is it true?"

He looked up at the door and saw her standing just inside, biting her lip with cautious excitement in her eyes. He couldn't help but close the distance between them and gripped her upper arms. "We're gonna bring your girl home, sweetheart."

He saw her lip wobble and heard the hiccup in her voice and lost the battle he was fighting to keep a distance between them. He hauled her to his chest and held her, burying his head in her hair, and holding her tight while she cried.

He'd do anything to take away the pain and tears, but he knew she needed this outlet, to let her emotions go so she wouldn't implode. At least these were tears of relief and not the soul-sucking grief and guilt she'd been carrying.

Once her sobs abated, he held her away so he could see her face. "Better?"

Adeline nodded as he lifted the bottom of his shirt and wiped her tears from her cheeks. "I ruined your shirt."

"Sweetheart, I'm beginning to think you've ruined me for all other women."

Her eyes went wide at his words and then he saw the heat, the mirroring need, and his body tightened. God, he wanted her. He felt like a drowning man, and she was his island, his sanctuary.

"We need to go pack." He took her hand and led her out the door to his car.

He shot a text to Gunner who'd ensure the equipment made it to the plane. They drove in silence to his place, that after only a day with her in it already felt more like a home than ever before.

They were bringing her daughter home, but what then? Would she leave before they even had a chance to see if the chemistry they felt was real and lasting or would she stay? He didn't know if he'd be enough for a woman like Adeline. What could he offer her and Payton? Bad DNA and a few computer skills. His own father had chosen a life of crime over his family and even his mother had left when she'd gotten the fateful call from his father.

He glanced across the car and saw her eyes on him and his heart lurched. He was in love with a woman he'd barely kissed. For the first time in his life he knew he had his soulmate sitting beside him and he had no clue if he'd lose her.

CHAPTER TWELVE

ADELINE HAD SPENT a restless night in her new bed and had an ache between her legs she knew Javier could satisfy but he was holding back. She knew he was trying to be a good guy, to give her the space she needed but she needed him more. Over the weeks he'd become critical to her well-being, not as a friend but as someone she turned to for everything.

He was her friend, but he was also a man she couldn't stop fantasising about. Late at night when she lay in bed it was his body she imagined over her. His hands on her skin, burning a path of desire through her until she felt that heavy ache in her abdomen. His laugh and smile felt like a gift that made her heart clench in her chest.

When she felt weak, he somehow knew what she needed to stay strong, to keep the terror at bay and give her the strength she needed to carry on fighting. She'd felt so much shame falling for a man when her daughter was being held by Juan Ravelino, the man responsible for so much death and pain. Biding her time was the right thing, she knew that, without Jack or the others pointing it out to her, but it didn't make it any easier and Javier knew that and didn't try and convince her otherwise. He just allowed her to feel it all and held her when she fell apart.

Hearing about his past had been shocking, but it also filled in the gaps in the painting of his life story. Gaps that had stopped her from seeing the truth or blurred her image of him. His past still held him in its grip, and she wanted to ease that in any way she could. She'd been angry he'd lied but it hadn't lasted long. She knew she would've done the same thing in his position and would be a hypocrite to say otherwise.

The tension in the car grew as he parked outside his house, and she followed him inside. She'd spent the morning talking with Skye Jones, whom she'd met at the Easter egg hunt. They'd talked more about how Skye had gotten involved with her now-husband when her son was kidnapped. She'd admitted that it was while Noah was missing that she and Nate had taken things to the next level and she'd felt bad for feeling pleasure when her son was missing but without Nate, she wasn't sure she would've had the strength to get up in the morning. Relief had been sharp at the admission, the guilt she'd felt over her feelings toward Javier easing slightly.

Skye admitted that had it just been sex she never would've done it, but for her, it had been so much more. Nate was the love of her life, and she was his and it was how they expressed their togetherness. It was them against the world and it had made her stronger. Nate and his friends at Fortis Security had gotten Noah back and it had all worked out. Addie knew her feelings for Javier were more than sex or attraction, they shared a connection she couldn't put into words and maybe if she was lucky, she'd have the same outcome. It was something she prayed for every day.

Adeline knew how she felt about Javier, but she wasn't sure about his feelings for her. As he closed the door, she stood in the entryway, desperate to make the first move. He turned to look at her and suddenly she didn't have to. They were in each other's arms, his lips on hers, his tongue stroking deep as her hands tunnelled into his thick, soft hair.

He gripped her ass and lifted. Her legs wrapped around his waist as he backed her towards the door. Her hands gripped his shoulders, kneading the muscles beneath as he kissed his way down her neck, nipping at her collar bone. Adeline's head fell back, her breasts brushing his chest as he pressed the hard ridge of his cock against her clit through her jeans.

She rocked against him as her climax built quickly, both of them moving in a frenzy of touches and kisses.

"Oh, God, you're gonna make me come."

Javier groaned at her admission and rocked faster, his mouth descending on hers again as he kissed her in a hot, drugging display of dominance that turned her on. His hips flexed faster, and she needed more.

"I want to feel you inside me." Adeline reached between them and grabbed his belt, loosening it as she struggled with the button. He pushed her hand away and released his cock. Her hands were on him in a second, stroking the heated, steel flesh. This was wild and crazy, and she never wanted the feeling to end.

Javier dropped her feet and she whimpered at the loss of his body, her legs week from climbing that peak only to have him snatch it away. She saw him drop to his knees, his hands at her waistband as he undid the button and pulled her jeans and panties off in one go. She reached up and drew her shirt over her head, tossing it to the floor as she unhooked her bra. His eyes moved over her, the irises almost black with desire and lust. She felt like the most beautiful woman in the world when he looked at her like that, like a precious jewel.

"Jesus, you're perfect."

She reached for him as he lifted his arm over his head and pulled his shirt off, revealing the beautiful peaks and planes of muscle that made her mouth water. He lifted her again and her legs wrapped around him, her knees tightening on his hips as she felt the hard ridge of his cock at her entrance.

"Fuck, condom," he hissed against her throat, his lips doing wicked things to her.

"I'm on the pill and I'm clean."

His eyes drilled into hers, heavy with need and passion. "Are you sure? I'm clean but..."

Adeline knew sex without a condom made what they were doing that much more intimate and didn't care. She wanted to feel everything, to be a close to him as she could be. "I want to feel you."

His hand stroked her face as he kissed her cheeks, her eyelids, and finally her mouth as he eased inside her. Her head flew back, hitting the wall as the wonderful full feeling caused pleasure and pain to peek inside her, her pussy clenching around his length as he stilled, his cock inside her so deep.

Sweat dotted his brow, her fingernails dug into his shoulders as he began to move, slow at first, his hips rolling so his pubic bone rubbed her clit with a delicious friction that had her climax climbing at a heady speed.

The sounds he made, the words he whispered all coalesced when he began to slam into her harder and harder, his cock hitting that secret place inside her. Her orgasm hit her like an explosion, her breathing hitched and she cried out his name. Flashes of white sparked behind her eyelids and a pleasure unlike any she'd known before pulsed through her.

Javier never slowed, if anything he seemed to lose even more control and she fucking loved it. That she could evoke that kind of animalistic need in him drove her toward another climax, and as he shuddered through his, she felt her own rush through her.

Javier lifted his head, a sexy cheeky grin on his full lips. "I think I died."

Adeline laughed, a free feeling making her light as she held him tighter. "Don't you dare, I'm not nearly done with you yet." She didn't add that she feared she may never be done with him. This was new and they hadn't discussed what this even was and now there wasn't time.

"Did I hurt you?"

His hands flexed on her ass. She shivered with renewed need, her body wanting him again. "No, I loved it, it was perfect."

A look of regret which she understood crossed his face. They had to go, and she was glad of it because it meant she was getting her baby back, but she also wished they had more time.

"We need to clean up and get packed." He released her legs and eased out of her body, both of them wincing, their bodies sensitive from the almost violent lovemaking. "You take the main bathroom, and I'll use my en-suite."

He didn't ask her to join him, and it was probably for the best as they needed to get going but she still felt a stab of doubt assail her.

"Hey, we'll figure it out." He gripped her chin with his thumb and forefinger and kissed her slowly, her eyes fluttered shut at the languid kiss that was so sensual and tender. Javier pulled away and turned her toward the stairs, swatting her bare ass. "Go before I change my mind and drag you into my shower and devour you."

Adeline raced up the stairs, not because she didn't want him to do those things but because she did, and she knew they didn't have time.

Adeline showered quickly. Her body bore the marks of his touch and she admired them all, reliving every second of their encounter. After she'd showered, she quickly dressed in comfy jeans, a light pink tee, and a navy hoodie, lacing up trainers on her feet. Anxiety filtered through at the thought of facing Juan again and she knew everything was leading up to that.

It was why he'd taken Payton, to lure her out. Now she had confirmation her daughter was there she'd go and do whatever she needed to make sure her child was safe—even if that meant exchanging her life for Payton's. Astrid and Jack wouldn't allow it, but she didn't intend to ask permission. Payton was her daughter, and the choice was hers alone.

Lifting her bag, she walked to the door wondering if she'd see this room again. It had only been a day, but she already felt an emotional attachment to this place and this town, but most of all to the people who'd accepted her as one of their own. Then there was Javier, a wonderful, sweet man who'd nurtured her soul and brought her back to life and given her strength to face whatever she had to do next.

"You ready?"

Adeline startled and turned to look at him, hiding the melancholy she felt with a smile. He gave her a funny look and she knew she wasn't fooling him and hoped he put it down to nerves. "Yep, all set. Just checking I hadn't forgotten anything for Payton."

Javier took her hand, and she relished the warmth of his touch. He grounded her and made her feel safe in a way nobody ever had.

"Let's go get her back and then we can figure everything else out."

Javier locked up and gripped her hand as he walked her to the car and opened the door for her. He had old fashioned manners which she loved, and she wondered what kind of husband and father he'd be. She decided he'd be kind and attentive, strict yet loving, showing those he loved how special they were to him.

"Javier?"

"Hmm?" He glanced at her as he drove out of the town and houses were replaced by fields of green.

"What happens now? With us? Do you even want there to be an us or is this all you want?"

She didn't want to trap him or force him to make promises he wasn't ready for, but she needed to know how to proceed. She had to shore her defences, so she could focus on her child. She couldn't do that if she was wondering and doubting and trying to guess where she stood. She'd spent too much of her adult life trying to guess how to move forward.

"I don't want to pressure you. It's fine with me whatever this is, I just need to know." Adeline looked out of the window at the lambs in the fields, not wanting him to see how desperate she was for him to want her. She hated feeling pathetic and desperate. It made her feel week and nothing like the strong woman who'd fought her way back from the horror she'd suffered at Juan's hands.

Her attack and subsequent coma had taken a toll and she was still recovering emotionally even though her body was strong now. Perhaps having her daughter home and safe would help her feel like that person again.

The car began to slow, and she realised they'd reached the airfield as the car stopped and she saw Jack and Astrid talking to Will and Aubrey.

"Addie, look at me."

She twisted her head so she was looking at him and her heart stuttered at the fierce emotion she could see in his strong straight brow, and deep brown eyes.

"I want us to see where this goes. I've never felt this way about anyone before. You make me feel alive, as if everything is sharper, brighter. I want to get to know Payton and walk by the river in the summer with Payton on her bike and us eating an ice cream. But I can't offer you any guarantees. I'm not good at this. Every person I've ever loved has left me. It scares the living fuck out of me how much I want you in my life, but I want to try if you do." Tears pricked her eyes and she blinked as he reached across the centre console and cupped her cheeks. "I want us."

"I want that too, but I have to put Payton first. She's my priority and always will be."

"So she should be, and I don't want it any other way. I just want a corner of your life to share with you."

"Okay."

Javier smiled. "Okay? So does that mean you're my girl now?"

Adeline smiled. "I guess it does, yes."

"Then bring your ass closer so I can kiss you."

Addie obliged, allowing him to kiss her until her toes curled. Only the loud knock on the outside of the window had them remembering where they were.

Javier leaned his forehead against her shoulder. "Fucking Liam."

Adeline looked up to see a grinning Liam watching them.

For the first time since she'd regained consciousness, she felt hope for the future. She just needed to vanquish her demons.

CHAPTER THIRTEEN

Lopez had hardly taken his eyes off Addie during the flight and now, as they arrived at their destination on the outskirts of Mexico City, he wanted nothing more than to pick up where they'd left off. That wasn't an option, and he knew it. They had a shit tonne of work to get done and they needed to establish a safe base for the team.

He snagged her hand as they stepped into the large hacienda style house that was used as a holiday home by a friend of Jack's. The security was top of the range and had been designed and installed by Will as a favour after the man's son had been kidnapped by a crazy ex of the woman who was now his wife. Hunter McKenzie had offered the place as soon as he'd heard the situation they were facing.

Addie curled her fingers around his and leaned in as if wanting him close and he obliged, wrapping his arm around her shoulder and kissing her head. He wasn't usually one for PDA but with her it felt natural, and he didn't give a fuck what other people thought. He glanced around and realised nobody that mattered cared either.

"Right, everyone grab a room. Astrid and I will take the master suite and I assume by the lovey-dovey shit that Lopez and Addie have going on they'll be sharing as well. After that it's every man for himself."

Lopez chuckled as Waggs and Liam made a dash for the bedrooms. Reid and Gunner had stayed behind with Blake and Alex to keep an eye on Hansen and Einhorn. Everyone agreed he was a bigger threat than they'd first realised. Lopez would personally love a few minutes alone in a room with Hansen.

"Let's go before we get stuck with the couch." He took her hand again, her bag and his thrown over his shoulder. They reached a double room on the second floor at the opposite end to the master and he closed the door, dropping the bags on the floor.

Addie went to sit on the bed, and he watched her, trying to read her mood. She'd been quiet on the flight, which was no surprise given where they were headed, and that was without what had happened between them. He moved to sit beside her, giving her space but wanting to feel her skin under his more than his next breath.

Her fingers were clasped in her lap, and he took her hand stroking the palm. "You doing, okay?"

Adeline cocked her head. "Yes, I think so. It's weird being back here knowing Payton is so close but not being able to get to her."

He pulled her close so she was leaning against his side and put his arm around her. "I can't even imagine how you must feel. If I could swap places with you, I would in a heartbeat. Is there anything I can do?"

Addie shook her head, her hair rubbing against his cheek, the scent of her shampoo teasing his senses. "No, this helps though, just being with you."

"Yeah, well, that I can do." He lay back on the bed and pulled her across his chest so she was half lying over him, her leg thrown over his waist, her hand on his abdomen.

"You okay with us sharing a room? I know we had wild monkey sex and agreed to give this a go, but I don't want you feeling pressured when you have enough on your plate already."

Adeline looked up at him through thick dark lashes. "No, this is what I want. I feel safe when I'm with you. Like nothing can touch me or hurt me."

"You *are* safe Addie. I won't let anyone hurt you ever again." His lips captured hers and like lighting a fire, the kiss went from gentle to red hot in a second. Her hands tunnelled under his t-shirt, her fingers urgent as they feathered over his skin, making him groan as his muscles contracted.

He turned them so he was lying over her, his hands in her hair. He could taste the need in her kiss, feel the heat between her legs as he pushed his hard dick against the seam of her jeans. He caught her moan with his mouth as he rocked against her, hoping like hell he wouldn't embarrass himself by coming in his pants like a damn teenager.

"Don't stop."

"Not a fucking chance." He plucked at her nipple through the lace of her bra, causing her to arch her back, offering him more. Her leg came around his waist as she thrust her hips against his hard cock seeking the relief she knew he could give her.

Her breathing became frantic, her body freezing as she came without him ever touching her pussy. Just the two of them going at it like teens, dry humping and he fucking loved that she was so responsive to him. That he could ignite such a fire in her she let go and just felt what he could give her.

Lopez kissed her neck as she caught her breath, the taste of her skin the sweetest he'd ever known. He wanted to feast on every inch of her but knew he didn't have time. They needed to get set up and form a plan to meet with Shadow.

"I wish we could stay here all night, but we need to get downstairs before they send Liam up to get us again."

"What about you?"

"That wasn't for me, that was for you."

Addie ran her palm over his hard cock which was straining for relief, and he pulled his hips away not knowing if he could cope with her hands on him right then.

"What about this?"

"Ignore it and he'll get the message."

Adeline giggled. "Did you just refer to your dick in the third person?"

"Shh. You'll offend him." He kissed her lips and pushed off the bed, holding out a hand for her to take. He pulled her up and kissed her lightly. "You ready?"

He watched the worry move back into her features and wished for a time when he could erase all her fears and pain for good. He wanted to slay dragons for this woman, to fight beside her and protect her from anyone who would hurt her or Payton.

They headed back into the main area and saw Rafe talking to Jack, who looked up when they walked in the room. Waggs and Liam were talking to Mitch and Astrid, and Decker was standing beside the door looking out into the night.

"Rafe is going to handle the dogs for us when we storm the Ravelino mansion."

"Have we heard from Shadow yet?" Lopez let go of Addie and moved to his laptop. He needed to get set up and not act like a lovesick idiot, even if the truth was, he was one. The team moved in as if sensing information was forthcoming.

"Yes. We have a meeting with Bás and Bein tonight. I want you and Decker with me. Everyone else stays here. The likelihood is that Ravelino knows we're here already and although I don't think he'll attack we can't be too careful."

Jack walked up to Astrid who was now seated beside Addie, offering her silent support he was glad of. He wanted to be the one by her side for everything but the best way he could help her now was to do his job.

"Lopez, Duchess is going to send you footage from inside the Ravelino mansion. I need you to identify as many men as you can and get as much info as possible. Addie, I need you and Astrid to draw me a map as detailed as possible of the inside including any hidden passageways. Once we've met with Shadow, we'll form a plan for getting Payton out."

Lopez glanced at Addie when Jack said her daughter's name and saw her swallow. He knew she was struggling but she was pushing it all down to deal with after. She was a survivor and it only made him love her more.

The thought brought him up short. Was he in love with her? As he examined the feeling he had around her and when he looked at her or she crossed his mind, which was every minute of every day, he realised yes, he was in love with her. It had been so subtle in the happening that he hadn't seen it until now, when it was as much a part of him as breathing was.

His phone rang and he pulled it from his pocket. Seeing Reid's name he got a dull feeling of dread in his gut. "Hello."

"Lopez, put me on speaker."

Lopez looked up at Jack who was watching him. "It's Reid. He wants to be on speaker."

Jack nodded and Lopez placed the phone down on the side and hit speaker.

"Reid, this is Jack. What do you have for us?"

"Einhorn was just pulled out of the river. He had two gunshots. One to the head, one to the heart."

Lopez looked at Addie, trying to read her reaction as Liam swore a blue streak.

"What about Hansen?"

"We lost him, but Gunner and I agree this is him. He's cleaning house."

"Okay, keep me appraised of the situation and have Alex call me as soon as he can."

"Ah yeah, that's the other thing. Alex is at the hospital. Evelyn went into labour an hour ago."

Lopez felt his lips curve into a smile of happiness for his friend.

"Fine. Have Blake call me when you know more."

"Will do."

Reid hung up and Jack looked at him. "Lopez, tell me more about what you found on Hansen."

He swung back to his monitor and loaded up what he knew. "Hansen has several offshore bank accounts in shell names with a couple a million in them. He seems to get large payments every six months and two of them coincided with Addie and Astrid being burned. I haven't traced where the payments have come from yet but I'm working on it. He's linked to a case known only as Cradle. Most of it is redacted but it was set up six years ago and suddenly closed down shortly after, but I think it's actually still alive. I just need to find out the details, but my gut says it involves kids."

"It does." Addie stepped forward. "I forgot about it, but it was before our time and was set up as an experiment. They took young, unmarried mothers and offered to have their children adopted but the truth was they were raising those children to be operatives. Sent them to foreign countries as sleepers where they would grow up and live like anyone else and when they were activated, they'd work for the CIA as an asset."

"Jesus, how did we not know this?" Mitch snarled looking furious and Lopez understood it, he felt the same.

"Because it was shut down in the eighties."

"Well, it looks like it was started up again. I just don't know if it's being done via the CIA or if Hansen is involved in some other way."

Jack pointed at him. "Find out. I want this fucker shut down, permanently."

Addie looked at him, her face ashen. "Jesus, if he knows about Payton then he could have the same planned for her."

He stood and moved to her, pulling her into his body as she shook.

Astrid came close and laid her hand on her sisters back. "We won't let that happen, Addie."

"No, we won't. We'll meet with Shadow tonight and have her with you by this time tomorrow." Lopez kept his eyes on Jack, begging him not to make him a liar. His boss dipped his head acknowledging his silent plea and he breathed easier. Now they just had to figure out how Hansen and Ravelino were involved, and they were. He'd bet his house on it, he just had to figure out how.

CHAPTER FOURTEEN

"ANYTHING else you can remember or is that everything?"

Addie cast a glance over the drawing she and Astrid had made of the mansion. Her sister was an excellent artist as well as all her other gifts and as she walked through the Ravelino mansion in her mind she found nothing had been missed. "That's it unless anything has been added since you left."

Astrid cocked her head. "I agree and we can't exactly plan for the unknown, just that we have to be prepared for anything."

"Maybe this Shadow team can shed more light on things."

"Maybe." Astrid rolled the drawing and stood from the table where they'd been hunched over, arching her back and groaning. "I need a massage."

"You'd better go find that man of yours then."

Astrid looked at Jack with a look so filled with love Addie would've felt a slight tug of envy but instead, her gaze went to Javier. He was everything she'd never known she wanted. Sweet, sexy, clever, strong, and protective without being an overbearing asshole and he seemed to have an awareness about him, as if he always knew where she was in a room. It made her feel safe and cherished but not suffocated. Then there was the sex, that man knew what he was doing between the sheets and all it seemed to take was a look and she was wet for him. His hands and mouth had played her body like a violin. Just the thought made her pussy clench with a need like none she'd ever known before.

"I like him for you."

Adeline blinked and turned back to Astrid as a blush crawled up her neck. She'd been lost in thought and totally forgotten her sister was standing there. "I don't know what it is about him apart from he's obviously gorgeous, kind, and has the sexy geek with muscles thing going on but it's as if my soul recognised his when I woke up." Adeline felt the heat on her cheeks deepen, feeling silly for voicing her innermost thoughts when they were so fanciful. "That sounds stupid, doesn't it?"

Astrid rubbed her arm, forcing Adeline to look up at her taller sibling. "Not at all. I felt the same with Jack, it just took him longer to see it. Lopez sees it. If he's not all the way, then he's at least halfway in love with you."

Adeline gasped, her eyes moving back to him as he typed furiously at the computer. He'd set up three and linked them and some other equipment so it was like mission control. He must have sensed her watching because he lifted his head and turned to her, a smile curving his lips that made her stomach flip over.

She returned it and twisted back to Astrid. "No."

"Yes, and if I'm not mistaken, you feel the same way."

She could deny it, but she knew it was the truth. She was falling in love with him. "What if I fuck it up or he and Payton don't get along?"

"Addie, quit looking for problems. He and Payton will be fine. Lopez is great with kids, and you'll find your way but don't let fear stop you from taking this leap with him. He's a good man."

"Yeah, he is."

Astrid walked towards Jack, and she was left to consider what she'd said. She wanted a future that included Javier, but her daughter always came first. She just hoped for once the gods were smiling on her and she could walk away from this with everything she wanted.

She took a seat beside Javier as if pulled by an invisible force to him and smiled when he turned to her.

"All sorted?"

"Yeah, as much as we can remember anyway and obviously it doesn't include any changes he's made since."

Javier's hand landed on her thigh, and he squeezed gently. "It will help the team a lot. I know this isn't easy for you."

"No, it isn't but having you and Astrid here helps."

A warm look passed over his handsome face and she felt the heat of his touch and wondered at the need he'd awoken in her and if it would fade when the mission was over. She prayed that wasn't the case.

"So, I'm looking for leads on Hansen and thought we could go through the timeline again. A few things aren't adding up and I think it's a link between Juan Ravelino and Hansen. Want to help me?"

"Sure."

"Okay, let's start at the beginning." He brought up a screen that had the events and the timeline going back before Payton was taken. She felt bile in her throat at the thought of that day. "Talk me through what happened when Payton was taken again, and the days preceding that."

His hand was back on her leg, and she found it grounded her and helped her to focus on the facts and not the crushing pain she felt. "I'd dropped Payton off at school."

"The same one you work at?"

Adeline nodded. "Yes. I had a dentist appointment, so I had a free period after lunch. I saw her at lunch, and she waved at me across the classroom." Adeline swallowed remembering her daughter's confident carefree smile across the room. "I went to my dentist appointment."

"Did you notice anything out of the ordinary at all?"

Adeline shook her head. "No, I was always on guard for any tiny detail that seemed off and there was nothing. I had my check-up and polish and went to collect Payton but when I got there her teacher was frantic, saying she was missing. I lost it for a bit and then got a grip and had them check the CCTV footage. There was no sign of her at all. We called the police, but they were no help."

Adeline crossed her legs, her limbs feeling antsy as memories of the worst day of her life flooded her mind.

"Then what did you do?" Javier was stroking her knee, innocent touches not meant to be sexual but to calm her, and they did to a degree, but the terror of that day was like a living, breathing beast.

"I called Brand and got no answer, so I tried Hustle and it was the same. I figured they were on a dark mission. I knew it was Ravelino, my gut was telling me so. I'd been keeping an eye on Astrid via a few tricks I learned in the agency and knew I had to ask for her help."

"So, you flew to Canada, and then what?"

"I followed her, but it was hard to get close without you guys seeing me, so I got an invite to the school via my teachers' association membership. I knew if Astrid saw me she'd know I needed her."

"Then you left the note."

Addie dipped her head. "Yes, I needed her help. I was terrified of dragging her into it, but I was desperate. You have to understand, Payton is my baby. She's my world."

"Hey, nobody is judging you. You did the right thing, and some would argue you should've done it sooner."

"I judge me, Javier. Don't you get it? I put my sister and all of you in danger because I'm selfish."

Javier grabbed her hand and towed her toward the room they were sharing, and she let him, shame and regret a bitter pill to swallow. He pushed her to sit on the bed and took the space beside her, not leaving any room between them as he faced her, his hands on her knees.

"Listen to me, Adeline, none of this is your fault. You did what you thought was the best thing at the time to protect your daughter. I don't think any one of us would've done things differently. You're a good mother and a wonderful human being and I, for one, think you're the least selfish person I know."

He cupped her neck and she felt tears spill over. He caught them with his thumbs before pulling her to his chest and holding her tight. Adeline let the tears fall silently and soaked up the strength of the man who was becoming her everything.

"Tell me what happened at the warehouse, sweetheart?" His voice was soft, coaxing not demanding she tell him, but telling her she was safe.

"I made a base there as it was close to the docks. Because it had a high crime rate I knew I could go under the radar. I must have dozed off because I was woken by a fist to the face and then it's a blur. I think there were two of them, but I lost consciousness pretty quickly. I guess you guys found me."

His arms squeezed tighter, and she knew the state she'd been in when they found her and that she was lucky to be alive. Without them she'd be dead and her daughter would be lost for good.

"Here's the thing, this doesn't fit."

Adeline pulled away to look at Javier, his arms still cradling her. "What doesn't?"

"Well, Payton goes missing and you reach out to Brand. When you have no luck, you look for Astrid but if Ravelino has Payton, why did Iago and his men go after Astrid on the beach with Jack? They said they were looking for you, but they knew where you were, so either they lied or—"

Adeline sat up. "Or Juan didn't have her." She felt her eyes go wide as she slapped a hand over her mouth to stop the panic.

"Exactly. Is it possible Hansen knows she's his daughter and he took her?"

"I don't see how."

"Do you trust Brand and his team?"

"Absolutely. Without them I'd be dead."

Javier stood and paced, pushing his hands through his hair. "We're missing something. We know Ravelino has Payton now, but he may not have been the one to take her. If I had to bet, I'd say Hansen took her and made a deal with Ravelino."

"Do you think he'd hand over a child if he believed she was his?"

Adeline thought back to the man who'd seduced her and left her to die. Could he have handed Payton over if he thought she was his? She didn't think so. He was a control freak, and a child would be leverage. "No, I don't think so."

"We need to find Hansen and figure out how he found you and what he's involved with."

"But Reid and Gunner lost him."

Javier grinned. "Nobody stays lost from Eidolon for long." He glanced at his watch. "I need to go meet with Shadow, but can you work with the others on this while I'm gone? I'll explain to Jack and Decker."

"Yes, of course." Adeline felt a surge of adrenaline and love for the man who was piecing her life back together for her. She stepped forward and kissed him hard, her hands threading through his hair. "Be careful. You mean the world to me."

He ran his thumb along her bottom lip. "Ditto, baby."

CHAPTER FIFTEEN

DECKER GLANCED around as the car Jack was driving slowed close to the meeting spot. "I fucking hate this place."

Lopez stayed quiet but agreed, The La Joya a.k.a. El Hoyo had one of the highest crime rates in the city with more cases of rape and violence against women than any other. Fortunately, the people here didn't want attention any more than they did, so it was the perfect meeting spot for Shadow, whose identities were shrouded in secrecy. It was also only thirty minutes from the Ravelino mansion which was in the affluent area of Polanco and a twenty-minute drive from where they were staying.

"Do you really think Hansen is the person who took Payton?" Jack caught his gaze in the rear-view mirror and although it was dark, he could feel the anger emanating from his boss that he himself felt towards the man who'd hurt the women they both loved.

"I do. It fits with what happened in Canada. They found Astrid after Payton was taken, so they didn't know where Adeline was."

"Do you think Ravelino just wants Adeline because she made a fool of him, or because he believes Payton is his child?"

Lopez glanced at the window, watching the darkness, and noting the eyes on them. "I don't know. Payton is blonde like Astrid so I can't believe Juan Ravelino would believe she's his, but you never know with a man like him. My gut says he wants Adeline to punish her for making him look like a fool."

"Did you tell Adeline this?"

Lopez's eyes shot to Decker who'd asked the question. "God no. She'd lose her mind because as far as Addie is concerned, he won't hurt Payton because he believes she's his. If I tell her my fears, she'll lose that security and she needs it right now."

"Hansen would sell his grandmother for a pizza so I wouldn't put it past him to use his own child to get what he wants from Ravelino."

"Piece of shit needs to be buried." Lopez struggled to contain his anger.

"Heads up." Jack began to move, and Lopez almost jumped when he saw a man peering inside the car. He hadn't seen him coming, not even in the glass and if Decker's reaction was anything to go by, neither had he.

"Fucking hell, where did they spring from?"

Jack smirked as he exited the car. "Told you they were good."

Lopez followed, putting his back to the wall as he took in the two men and one woman. He knew Bás from previous missions and that he was involved with the shit that went down with Jack's father and Gunner. The other man was tall, probably six feet four and muscular, tattoos covered his neck and hands. Sharp, pale blue eyes were scanning the area for threats and Lopez got a definite military vibe from him but also a wildness that he couldn't put his finger on. His short, reddish-blond hair was lighter than his beard, which showed more of the red, but it was tidy and short. A scar ran through his brow and a tiny tattoo that looked like a thistle was high on his cheekbone near his left eye. Everything about him was a warning not to get too close and Lopez was glad he was on their side.

The woman was watchful and had the same vibe as Roz, the Zenobi leader, almost angry and cold. She wouldn't tolerate bullshit and could probably maim a man and draw blood without lifting a finger. She was beautiful with long dark hair, wide grey-green eyes, and full lips. She also had tattoos on her neck and one arm. She was a walking temptation, yet he felt nothing except a passing appreciation for a stunning human being.

Adeline was more beautiful in every way as far as he was concerned, and he realised again how far gone he was for her.

"Bás, Bein, Duchess, this is Lopez, and you know Decker from your assessments."

Lopez nodded at the newcomers.

"What have you got for me?" Jack didn't beat around the bush.

"Ravelino has security on alert and my bet is he knows you're here. The dogs are patrolling, and they moved the kid into the room next door to Juan Ravelino." Bein was watching the area around him as he spoke, his body tense as if expecting an attack. Bás seemed calmer, more relaxed but Duchess looked ready for a fight, her lip curling as she looked across the road at a man loitering near the corner of a dive bar.

"He most likely knows we're here, but we expected that. He has so many officials on his payroll my guess is nobody gets into this city without him hearing about it."

Bein smiled, a slow grin. "You want him watching you so a small team can slip in behind. You're a distraction."

Lopez thought he detected a Scottish bur in Bein's voice but wasn't sure.

"Yes, but I need you to keep eyes on him at all times. We think he'll use the child to bargain with."

"Mother fucker," Bás hissed, his fists clenching.

Lopez had come to realise over the last year that there wasn't a lot the new leader of Shadow wouldn't do to get the job done but he drew the line at harming kids.

"Duchess, you've been with Payton. How is she?"

Lopez's heart kicked up a gear and he thought he saw the woman soften but it was so fleeting it was there and gone before he could identify it.

"She's a freaking warrior. She misses home but she's being cared for by the housekeeper, who's lovely and quite protective of her."

"Do we have a name for her?"

"Mia. She's probably in her mid-fifties, but I haven't got much more than that." Duchess began to unzip her jacket and Lopez turned to look behind him, wondering what had made her do it and saw the man across the street watching her with a little too much interest.

"Time to go." Jack opened the car door. "Find out if she's an ally or can be turned. We're getting the kid out tomorrow. Ravelino has a shipment of drugs coming in and we're going to make sure they disappear or go boom. That will give you time to slip in when the guards are distracted and rescue Payton."

"That's a risk in broad daylight."

"I know but we're running out of time, and we lost Hansen. We can't have him involved or this turns to shit."

"We should handle the shipment and you get the kid." Bás seemed worried about his team being outed.

Decker glared at Bás. "You know the mansion layout better than us. It makes sense, and we have Pyro."

"Stop fucking arguing," Jack growled. "Lopez, me, Rafe, and Waggs will be here and do the retrieval and you watch our backs. Pyro, Astrid, Deck, and Mitch can handle the shipment."

"Fine."

"Glad you're happy, Bás, that's literally the main focus of my fucking day." Jack got in the car and Lopez and Decker followed, Decker and Bás still glaring at each other. "Wait for my call."

Jack put the car in drive and before they'd even moved, Shadow had disappeared as if they'd never been there in the first place. Lopez was impressed and that took a lot. After working with Eidolon for so long he'd thought he was immune.

"How come Astrid won't be with you, Jack?"

Lopez wondered that too as Decker glanced at his boss as he

drove through the dark streets of the poorer areas of Mexico City that sat just outside the luxury of the tourist area and the rich.

"Astrid and I agreed we'd limit working together on things like this. It's one thing when we're doing work for the Queen but on something like this, she'll distract me as my focus will be on her safety and not the job. I trust Mitch and Liam and you," he gave Decker a hard look of warning, "to keep her safe. Plus, she's a force all on her own and I need to try and keep that in mind."

Lopez respected his boss for his decision. He knew it wasn't an easy one, but it *was* the right one and Jack always put Eidolon first. "What about Adeline, Jack? You can't bench her. This is her kid we're talking about."

"I know. She'll be with us, but you're in charge of keeping her under control. If she goes off-book, she'll blow it and we could all end up dead. She does as I fucking say, or she stays back at the base with a babysitter. I won't have my woman grieving her sister's death a second time."

And there was the overprotective partner, although he understood it. He'd want Adeline out of the line of fire if he had the choice, but he knew doing that would show her he didn't trust her and that was so far from the truth. The fact was, he couldn't imagine how he was going to feel with her being in the line of fire and yet he had no other option. What he'd said to Jack was the truth—they couldn't expect her to sit it out when it came to Payton.

Seeing her guilt over the risks she'd asked them to take and the target she'd put on Astrid almost slayed him. His initial interest in her had been about his mother but as time had gone on and he'd sat by her bed willing her to wake up, that had faded until it was almost an afterthought now. He'd always want the truth about his mother and what happened to her, but he no longer looked at Adeline as his ticket to the truth. No, she was so much more, she was his future.

He loved her and he wanted what his friends had, a family, someone to come home to, to curl up with at night and talk about random nonsense. A woman he could build a life with who'd stand beside him. He hadn't known he wanted that until Adeline and now it was the only thing he wanted from his life.

His mind drifted to Alex, and he wondered if his friend was a father yet and if he'd ever get that chance. To give Payton, a child he'd never met but who'd made a space for herself in his heart because of who she was and the stories her mother told him about her, a sibling. A little boy with Adeline's eyes and his aptitude for tech or a little girl with curly dark hair and a cheeky smile who loved science.

He rubbed his chest where the ache for that dream resided. All of this hinged on so many small things that could go wrong but he had to have faith and belief like his mother had taught him. Her gift to him was to always believe you could, and to treat the brain like a computer, if you programmed it correctly, the rest would follow.

He knew that wasn't always the case, but he got the lesson she'd tried to give him—that self-belief and positive energy were key to certain things. He'd do his job and bring Payton home and then he'd convince Adeline they had a future to build and ask her to trust in what they felt, and the rest would hopefully fall into place.

CHAPTER SIXTEEN

"ADDIE, will you please stop pacing and sit down." Adeline heard the worry in her sister's voice and sat on the white leather couch beside her. Astrid's hand landed on her arm, and she saw the raised brow. "You're going to make yourself ill with all this worrying."

"I'm fine, I just want to know what news they have of Payton."

Adeline loved her sister dearly, but she wasn't sure she quite understood the crippling fear of not having her child with her, or the guilt she carried. She was a mother, and her job was to protect her child and she hadn't, it was a simple as that.

A car drew up and she was on her feet, heading for the door before it had even stopped in the gated driveway. This house was ridiculously secure, and she wondered again who owned it, but it was a fleeting thought. Her eyes scanned the screen where a camera captured anyone coming near the house. Finally, her gaze landed on Javier, and she let out a sigh of relief she hadn't realised she was holding.

Stepping back, she let Jack step through with Decker and Javier behind them. Her arms were around him before he could make it past the entranceway. Strong arms encircled her and held her tight to his body as she buried her head in his neck, taking in the scent that settled her and made her body light up with desire.

Javier set her back so he could see her face but didn't let her go and she was glad of it. "What's all this?"

"Nothing. I'm just happy to see you."

He dipped his head slightly so he could see her eyes, his assessing her and looking for a truth he knew was there. "I'm fine and so is Payton."

Addie gripped his forearm as he steered her towards the living room where his computers were set up. He eased into an easy chair and pulled her onto his lap, holding her close.

"Tell me," she demanded needing the words, any tiny bit of information about her child.

Her hand rubbed his arm, and she didn't know if it was to soothe him or her. Her whole body quivered; a ball of anxiety sat like lead in her belly. It was almost a constant now she was so used to the anxiety.

His features softened, his brows drawing together. "Payton is well and healthy. She's being cared for by Ravelino's housekeeper."

"Mia?"

"Yes."

Addie looked to the ceiling, a breath trembling between her lips in relief. Mia was a good, kind woman who'd been nothing but sweet to her. Addie had never asked for her help, knowing she had her own demons to deal with and there was no way a woman as sweet as her was there by choice.

"She was lovely. Quiet but kind and an amazing cook. She always looked sad though, as if she'd had all the fight taken from her."

"Do you know her surname or anything else about her?" Javier's hand rubbed her thigh as she leaned into him, listening to his heart beat and feeling it calm her shattered nerves.

Addie shook her head. "No, we didn't really interact. She was sweet when we spoke, but I got the feeling she was as trapped as I was, and I didn't want to call attention to her. But I got a good vibe from her."

"How old is she?" His voice was low, his breath feathering her hair.

"Hard to say but I'd guess around sixty."

"That's good."

"When are we going to get her back, Javier?" His arms tightened and she stilled, worrying they'd try and shut her out. She sat up and looked at him steadily. "Don't even think about leaving me here. I may not be at my peak fitness, but I'm as trained as you are, and I know my way around any weapon."

She felt her blood rush through her ears when he smirked, his sexy mouth tipping into a grin. "This is not funny." She made to stand, and he held her tighter, his arms locked tight around her body, and she squirmed.

"Addie, stop and listen to me."

She wasn't used to him being so firm, or his voice being so growly, and despite the fact she was ready for a fight over this she felt her body react with desire to the dominant command. Her body stilled and her breathing sped up and the squirm became less about getting away than feeling the hard ridge of his cock beneath her ass. She wouldn't let this go though, no matter how much she wanted his hands on her.

"Addie, quit fucking wriggling and listen to me."

She folded her arms in defiance and to hide the fact her nipples were hard from his searching eyes. "Fine."

"Good. Now, as I was saying, we, as in me, Jack, Rafe, and Waggs will be going into the Ravelino mansion tomorrow at midday to do the retrieval. Shadow will be watching our backs. Pyro, Astrid, Deck, and Mitch will be at the docks using the shipment as a distraction by setting some explosions. You'll be with me at the house, but you have to do as Jack says. He's running this, and he's fucking good at what he does, but if you go off book and lose your head, then one of us will end up dead."

"I can take orders."

Javier stroked her cheek softly, the rough of his fingers welcome against her skin. "I know you can, sweetheart, but this is Payton and I know when it's someone you love all bets are off. That's why Astrid will be at the docks with the others because they both know it makes sense."

"What about us?"

Javier frowned in confusion, and she wanted to snatch the words back before he asked for clarification of what she meant. She hadn't meant to say the words out loud, but they'd popped out.

She made to move, and he let her go as she put space between them. It was almost three in the morning, and she should be exhausted, but her body was wired. Yet, there was nowhere to go and she knew going to bed was her only escape. "We should get some rest."

Addie made it to the bedroom they'd share thinking she had gotten away with her slip up but should have known better. Javier missed nothing, none of these men did. She felt his heat behind her as he closed the door quietly behind them.

"Adeline." His voice was deep, gravel and cut glass and her pussy clenched at the deep dominance she could hear.

"I'm tired." She began to pull her pyjamas out of her bag. His voice was close when he spoke again and her heart beat so loud, she was sure he could hear it in the silence of the room.

"Adeline, look at me."

She turned and her breath hitched inside her chest. His cheeks had slashes of red across the defined bone structure, his eyes intense, the pupils dilated with need and his feet were spread, hands clenched at his sides.

Her mouth flooded with saliva, the hair on her neck rising in awareness as her body tingled. She couldn't have looked away if she'd tried.

He walked toward her slowly, every step making her heart beat harder until it felt like her chest would explode from all of the feelings inside her.

"Take off your shirt."

Javier had never ordered her around and she'd never been a woman to let a man tell her what to do, but this was different. He was the man she felt more for than any other man before, a man she loved and trusted with the softest part of her.

Her hands moved to her buttons, and she undid them, his eyes remaining on her face the whole time. Her shirt was tossed to the floor, and she stood in her jeans and bra, her chest rising and falling fast.

"Now the bra."

Addie unclipped her bra and slid the straps down, letting it fall to the floor. He never touched her, and she ached to have his hands on her, to feel him.

His eyes moved over her body and every place they touched prickled with need, her nipples hard as nails, goosebumps on her belly as need surged.

"Get on your knees, Addie."

She could see the hard line of his cock through the trousers he wore as she dropped to her knees, her mouth-watering with the urge to taste him.

"Good girl." His hand caressed her face and moved her hair back from her shoulders so he could pinch the tight peaks of her nipples, rolling them between his finger and thumbs.

"Take my cock out."

Addie was glad she was on her knees, the controlled desire making her weak and dizzy. She lowered the zipper and freed his cock, curling her hands around the silken skin that housed the hard length of him. Precum beaded on the tip, showing how much he was enjoying this. She was so wet her panties were soaked and she could smell the desire in the room.

"Suck me."

His words weren't in any way flowery, but they were hot. She closed her eyes and sucked the tip of his dick into her mouth, tasting the salty desire. Her eyes flashed open when he gripped her hair in a tight, almost painful, hold that seemed to intensify everything she was feeling.

He was watching her mouth, dark eyes like a predator, dangerous and lethal, and yet so compelling she couldn't look away. His breath hissed as she took him deeper, her own pleasure at this act making her ache to touch herself and ease the ache in her belly to fill the emptiness.

She licked and sucked, the noises wild as she moaned, and his hips pumped into her with less control now. His cock thickened and he pulled out, leaving her shocked.

"Fuck, Addie." Javier shed his shirt, pulling it over his head and dropping it to the floor as she removed his jeans. "Lose your jeans and panties and climb on the bed on your hands and knees."

Adeline did as he demanded and waited, her anticipation high, wetness coating her thighs with how turned on she was.

He swiped a finger through her labia, slowly gathering the wetness as he pushed a finger inside her. She knew it wouldn't take a lot for her to climax, just a couple of touches and she'd be gone.

"You're fucking soaked. Is this for me?"

Her eyes found his as she looked over her shoulder at him, loving the heat she saw directed her way. "Yes."

"Fuck me."

He gripped her hips and was balls deep inside her in one stroke. The pinch of pain coupled with the fullness of his cock had her pussy clenching, her body on the edge of orgasm.

"You feel like fucking heaven. I'm never gonna want to let you go."

"Then don't."

She knew the words exposed too much but she was too far gone to care.

Javier began to move, his hips hitting her ass as he fucked her hard and fast. Her first climax hit after two hard strokes and she cried out, her body tightening around his cock as he continued to fuck her through it. He didn't stop as she fisted the sheets and turned, seeking his mouth and he kissed her, it was messy and without any finesse and perfect in every way. His fingers found her clit as he angled his hips, hitting her secret spot and she saw stars as another climax, stronger than any before it, hit her, leaving her panting and screaming his name and she felt his seed spill inside her.

His heat and weight blanketed her back and she fell to the bed, having no energy to think of moving, content to stay where she was.

"We didn't use anything again."

"I told you I'm on the pill and I want to feel you," she mumbled not upset that they'd had sex without a condom again. This felt more intimate with his seed inside her.

He moved off her body, his climax coating her thighs as she rolled to her back before he pulled her into his chest.

"Is it caveman of me to say I like the idea of my cum inside you?"

Adeline laughed. "Yes, but I don't mind." She snuggled closer her hand on his chest. "But you get to sleep in the wet bit."

His chuckle filled her with warmth as he kissed her head, his arms wrapped tightly around her. "Addie."

"Yeah."

"I love you." Adeline held her breath at Javier's words, not wanting to break the spell and realise this was a dream. "Say something."

"Is this real?" He pinched her ass and she giggled. "Hey."

"Just showing you it's real."

"I love you too, Javier. I think I fell in love with you a while ago but was too confused to see it or acknowledge it. Then there's Payton. She's my world and falling in love while she's lost feels wrong and yet you feel so right. We feel right."

"I know the timing sucks, but we'll get through it. I'm not going anywhere, and we can take this as slow as you like. Just know that I love you and I want it all with you. A life, a family, a dog, a home."

"I want that too."

"Then we will have it. Let's start by getting Payton back where she belongs."

"Okay."

Her body relaxed against him, and she was just dropping off when a text alert came through and the screen beside Javier lit up.

"Who is it?"

He was silent while he read the message and smiled, turning the screen towards her and showing her the image of a beautiful baby with dark hair and her father's eyes.

"Alex and Evelyn have a daughter."

"I'm so happy for them."

"Me too, Addie, me too."

CHAPTER SEVENTEEN

The drive to the Ravelino mansion was quiet, the tension in the vehicle almost palpable. It felt strange to be heading on a mission when the sun was so high in the sky. Usually this would be done under the cover of darkness, but they'd changed up the rule book for this one and if Jack thought it was the best play, then it was. Pyro and his team had left earlier for the docks to make sure they were in position before it got busy and more eyes would be on them.

He'd felt a pang in his chest watching Jack and Astrid murmuring softly to each other before they left, understanding for the first time what his boss must be feeling. He hadn't expected to tell Adeline he loved her so soon, but he was glad there were no games between them. Things had escalated quickly in the last few weeks, but his mother had been right. When you met the right person, you knew.

He'd known for a while what he was feeling but had shied away from putting a name on it, not willing to recognise it when he'd been so torn regarding his father. Now he felt more settled, or he would when they had Payton back. He glanced at Addie as she watched the scenery go by, feeling the anxiety emanating from her in soft ripples. He wanted to reach out and pull her into his arms and tell her it would all be okay, but he had no way of knowing that would be the case.

If he had his way, he would've made her stay at the house, safe and away from the certain danger they were walking in to. Shadow had contacted Jack earlier to say that all was quiet, but Lopez wasn't convinced. He had a bad feeling in the pit of his gut, a growing knot of dread that wouldn't go away. Everything seemed too easy. Juan Ravelino knew they were in the city, of that there was no doubt, but he hadn't approached them in any way and no scouts had been spotted near the house they were sharing.

Liam, Rafe, and Deck had been out and around the area, checking for anything that was out of place and found nothing. They knew from their intel that Juan Ravelino was overseeing more of the shipments since his brother had been taken into custody by them for an attempt on the Queen's life. They also knew there were rumblings of unrest from inside the cartel and that other powerful families were flexing their muscles.

That played into their favour, causing Juan to have his attention on multiple areas of his operation at once and spreading his men thin. They still didn't know how Hansen fit for sure or why Juan was so determined to get Addie back. It could be simple pride, or maybe he believed Payton was his and that Addie would follow. His gut said that was the case, they'd found no evidence that Ravelino was involved in anything nuclear. He was strictly drugs, guns, and human trafficking. He was a despicable piece of shit for sure, but he had no evidence that he was involved in nuclear arms.

Which begged the question as to why Hansen kept sending women undercover into the Ravelino mansion. They needed Hansen, and the last he'd heard from Gunner was that they'd picked up his trail in Portsmouth. There were too many unknowns, and he didn't like it one bit.

The terrain began to change as they got closer to the mansion, the houses were further apart and the affluence and money clear compared to the children running barefoot not ten miles away.

Shadow was going to stay watching the house and they'd leave the vehicle and walk the last mile to the property.

The sun blazed down on his face as he exited the car, and he was glad they were wearing desert green camouflage rather than the usual black tactical gear. He stretched his neck, loosening his muscles. He was usually in the van for the actual mission but on this one he was going in with the rest of them. He was as trained as any of the other men and ran drills with them every week. Eidolon worked because despite them all having a speciality, they could all step in and do each other's jobs when required.

Jack reasoned that Addie would more than likely listen to him if the shit hit the fan for any reason on the ground, hence the reason he was geared up for war like the rest of them. This wasn't his first rodeo by any stretch, but it felt like the most important because something precious was on the line. He wasn't sure Addie would listen to anyone when it came to Payton, but he didn't say that to Jack.

"You doing okay, Addie?"

She was hiking beside him to the meet point, Waggs and Jack in front with Rafe moving in behind them. It would be Rafe's job to assess the animals and handle any sedation in a humane way. Will would handle comms remotely for him and he was glad to have him there. Shadow would cover their backs inside the mansion.

"I just want this done."

Lopez took a drink from his water bottle as they kept to the trees and cover, before offering it to Addie, who shook her head. "It can't be easy going back in there after everything he did to you." They'd talked about Juan and the way he'd controlled and hurt her, and he'd love just five minutes with the man to show him exactly how it felt to be powerless and in pain.

"It's fine. There's nothing I won't do for my daughter."

She sounded determined and fierce, but he could detect the apprehension. He let her have that for now. She needed to feel strong in this moment.

"I know."

"I'm glad you're here, Javier."

The sound of his name on her lips never failed to affect him and now was no different. He felt an overwhelming rush of love for her but underneath that, a cold slice of fear and alarm held him tight in its grasp.

They stopped half a click from the house and Jack scouted the area with his binoculars. "Shadow is in position, and everything seems quiet. Rafe, I need you behind the north wall where the kennels are and ready to go on my command."

Rafe nodded and took off at a steady clip. The man was fit and his background in the Royal Marines made him a perfect fit for the group.

Lopez watched Jack tilt his head slightly and knew he was listening as Pyro gave him an update on the other end.

"Charges are set and the shipment is just arriving. I bet we have maybe five minutes before the first charge blows and then another three before Juan rolls out of here. Let's get in position."

As previous recon and intel from Shadow had revealed, the north wall was the only weakness, which was why when they got the signal from Rafe they'd go in through the kennels. They ran, crouched low until just outside the line of the cameras set up all along on the north side. Will would knock them out for a few seconds to allow Rafe inside and loop them, so the guard wouldn't have a clue.

"Javier!"

He felt Addie's hand on his thigh as they stayed low, and his muscle tensed. "Yes?"

"Be careful in there okay. I couldn't forgive myself if you got hurt doing this for me."

He looked at her fully then, her cheeks were pink, but the rest of her face was pale, the fear evident in the tight line of her body and the way she whispered the words.

"Nothing is going to happen to me or you. We're going to get Payton out and go home and I'll introduce you both to my fried banana and chocolate spread sandwich." He saw her eyes crinkle in a smile which was what he'd intended. "Just make sure you listen to Jack. I love you, Addie." He kissed her but it was quick and nothing like the kiss he wanted to give her.

"Okay, it's go time. The charges have blown."

Lopez listened intently, feeling the hum of tension from Waggs and Jack. They were now all on the same frequency with Shadow but only Jack had access to Pyro's team at the docks. It didn't take long for the vehicles to start rolling out from the front gate where Bás was situated.

"I have eyes on Ravelino's car but not on him."

Lopez glanced at Jack. They both knew the chances were fifty-fifty this was a trap, but they had no choice.

"Are his men there?"

"Yes, all his usual guards are there."

"Will?"

"I have six heat signatures inside."

"Rafe?"

"Dogs are taking a nice long nap."

"Then we go."

Jack was up and moving with Lopez and Addie next, and Waggs following at the rear. Jack went over the wall first and helped pull Addie over and Lopez joined them with Waggs landing silently behind him. The guard dogs were all out cold and locked inside their cages. Rafe fell in behind as they kept to the left side of the garden which offered the most cover.

A pop sounded just in front of Jack, and they stopped as they saw four men coming out of the pool house dripping wet.

"Fuck, Jack, I didn't see them. You have eight men coming at you from the pool area." Will sounded calm but pissed off. The water had hidden the heat signatures from the infrared.

Jack waved his arm. "Lopez, Addie, go get Payton. We'll take care of this."

Lopez paused for a split second before he took off toward the house. His friends were outnumbered but they were far from out.

Pushing through the heavy door to the kitchen he saw a man dressed in black turn to them and raise his gun. Lopez dropped him where he stood, two bullets hitting his centre mass and head. He kept moving knowing Addie was covering his back as they cleared the place room by room, heading towards Juan Ravelino's office.

"Lopez, I see three heat signatures in the office and one in the hallway close to the stairs."

Lopez listened as Will talked him through what he could see and picturing it in his mind's eye. This was usually his role, but he needed to be there today. It was a feeling he couldn't put his finger on, a compulsion almost.

He glanced around the door into the hallway, with the opulent paintings and priceless art, and found it clear. The firefight outside was still going strong and it sounded like a war zone now. More men had appeared from the pool house and Shadow had moved to clear house, pinning the attackers between them and Eidolon.

As he and Addie turned the corner heading toward the room where they now knew Payton was being held, they heard shouting and a bullet almost hit him. He returned fire and managed to take the shooter down with a torso shot. Addie took out the next guy who appeared from Juan Ravelino's office.

"We need to clear these other rooms before we move on."

Addie nodded and they began to clear the rest of the rooms one at a time. As they got closer to the office where Payton was, he could hear a child crying and knew Addie did too by the distraught yet hopeful look on her face. A crying child was an alive child, and they both needed that.

They moved either side of the door and he counted in his head to calm the pounding of his heart. The likelihood was the last three heat signatures were in there, and while they could be friendly they were most likely foe.

"Ready?"

Addie's eyes met his and he saw the determination in them as she gave a short nod.

"Execute, execute, execute."

He knew the team would know they were moving into the retrieval part of the operation when they heard his command.

He slammed through the door, the wood giving against his shoulder, his weapon raised, eyes scanning the room for Payton and any threat and stopped dead. His eyes moved from the child curled on the floor to the woman behind her, watching him with a mixture of joy and sorrow on her familiar face. The woman he'd loved for as long as he could remember, the woman who'd raised him—his mother. That two seconds of shock was all it took for Juan Ravelino to pull the trigger. Pain ripped through his shoulder, and he staggered as another bullet tore through his thigh, causing his leg to give out beneath him.

Lopez lifted his gun with an arm heavy with pain but Addie beat him to it. She shot Juan in the arm as he twisted away but not before he grabbed Payton and dragged the crying child in front of him, holding a gun to her head.

"No!"

He heard the anguish in Addie's voice as she rushed forward, her weapon held out to the side in surrender.

"Stay where you are, or she dies."

"No. Please, Juan."

"She's mine."

Things were becoming hazy now as he sank all the way to the ground. He needed to get to his mother, who by some miracle was alive and here in this hell, and Payton and Adeline away from Juan. He blinked hard as the room spun, the sound of soft crying coming from the child who watched her mother with hope. The bullets were still inside him and although most likely nothing vital was hit, he was bleeding like a stuck pig. His brain already feeling sluggish, the noise in the room and that of the comms in his ear making it hard to focus.

"Aww isn't this nice, it's a family reunion all around." Juan tightened his hold on Payton, holding his injured arm against his body. "Put the fucking gun down, Adeline. That's your name, right?

Adeline Lasson, the CIA mole who opened her legs to get the job done and enjoyed every second of what I gave her."

Lopez blinked hard, fury at the man's words and the implication said in front of a child giving him strength from a place deep inside him.

Addie laid her weapon on the ground and glanced at him as if trying to assess his injuries and he saw her swallow.

"Please, Juan, not in front of her. Let her go with Mia and we can talk."

He must look worse than he felt, and he felt pretty deathly. Mia, why was she calling his mother Mia? That wasn't her name. He knew he had maybe two minutes before he passed out from blood loss.

"No. Mia gets to stay and watch her son die." Juan glared at him, and Lopez had the sense to play dead, to make him believe he was no longer a threat. What he wanted was to tear him apart limb from limb.

"Juan, please. Just let her go, she's a child."

"You beg me? After you ran away from me and hid her from her father?"

Lopez moved a fraction, trying not to wince and draw Juan's attention from Adeline. His eyes landed on his mother who was edging between him and Juan and wanted to curse. She was going to get herself killed and he had so many questions, but mostly he just wanted to tell her how much he'd missed her.

"This is so perfect. I could not have planned it better. Mia gets to watch her son die, punishment for her husband betraying me, and then you get to watch her die before I kill you."

Lopez saw his mother's foot land on the gun he'd dropped when he was hit and went down. Her glance told him what she'd do, that oh so familiar smile making his heart ache.

"I ran because you hurt me, Juan." Addie didn't react to the threats of death or beg for her life; it wasn't her style to give up. She was buying him time, trusting he'd find a way and he would.

"You are nothing, a plaything. But she is mine, my child."

"How did you find us?"

Juan waved the gun around like a maniac and Lopez's gut clenched. "Hansen thinks he's clever. He sends girls in to get information to use against me in order to protect his little side gig but all he's doing is sending me more toys."

"What side gig?" Adeline kept her hands up in the air as she talked, moving infinitesimally closer each time he spoke.

"His little toy soldier project. I'm surprised he let me have my Niña but then he had little choice with the money I offered him."

"How did he find me?"

"I have no idea." He shrugged his shoulder, his large belly rippling with the movement.

Payton began to wriggle in Juan's hold. "Momma."

It was just what they needed. His mother kicked the gun across the floor to Lopez who grabbed it on instinct and fired at Juan as he turned, exposing his chest with the sudden movement. Addie dove for Payton and caught her daughter in her arms, and he sagged back to the ground, all his energy spent but it was okay because the people he loved were safe now.

Lopez felt soft hands on his face. "Oh, my son, my poor baby."

Lopez could hear words and names, but it was all a blur. All he knew was his mother and the woman he loved were safe as Waggs and Jack rushed into the room.

"I leave you for two minutes and this happens," Jack joked as Waggs got to work but he heard no more as he blacked out.

CHAPTER EIGHTEEN

"YOU NEED SOME HELP?" Addie bit her lip to hide the grin as Javier glared at her before stubbornly negotiating the steps of the private plane they'd travelled home in. The bullets in his shoulder and thigh had been removed and he'd been given a blood transfusion. Thankfully, there wasn't any permanent damage, but she still woke gasping for air at night, images of him covered in blood in her mind. She'd take him grouchy and contrary over pale and injured any day of the week.

Waggs and Rafe walked ahead of them towards the waiting vehicles that would take them back to Hereford. They hadn't really discussed how things would work when they were back, between his surgery and getting home there'd been very little time. It had been agreed though that Mia would stay with Javier and rightly so. Those two had so much to talk about and she could understand Javier's reticence. It was hard to believe the same woman who'd shown her kindness was the mother of the man she loved. It was almost fateful in some ways.

"Mommy, where will we sleep?"

"You and your mommy are staying with me, pipsqueak." Addie

glanced up at Javier who was watching her even though his words had been aimed at Payton. "That's if you want to."

Addie could see the unasked question in his warm brown eyes. He was quiet, and the PDA had been put on hold but how he felt was still evident to her. She felt a whoosh of relief in her belly that he hadn't changed his mind about them being together. She knew the reality of a child was very different from talking about one. If he'd changed his mind about her, she wouldn't have blamed him.

"I want to."

Javier reached for her free hand, and she gripped it tight, the familiar feel of his fingers entwined with hers grounding her. His easy acceptance of Payton and hers of him had surprised her, although she was unsure why. Payton was resilient and easy going and so was he. As it turned out, Payton had been treated extremely well by Juan and if that was the only thing she could ever ask of him, it would've been that. Mia had taken on much of her care, and she'd been told it was a vacation and her mother would join them soon.

Adeline would never be able to thank Mia for what she'd done, for protecting her child when she couldn't.

"Good. Let's get home. I have a hankering for a pie and chips from our local chippy."

The car ride was filled with chatter. Although Payton was happily wedged between her and Javier, with Mia riding up front with Reid who'd been sent to meet them, Payton and Mia had quite the bond and they chatted constantly.

Resting her head back she felt like she could take her first full breath in months. She felt the warm stare of the man she loved and turned to see him watching her, a thoughtful look on his face. His lips tipped up in a grin, but she could see he was hiding pain behind his façade of indifference.

Typical alpha male to pretend he was okay when he wasn't. She didn't ask, knowing he'd wave away her concern. Since he'd woken, his only thought had been for her and Payton, and to a lesser degree, Mia. Addie knew there was a huge discussion brewing between mother and son about the last few years and she'd be there for him when that happened.

Reid pulled up outside Javier's home and helped them with the few bags they had. He slapped Javier on the shoulder making him flinch in pain and Reid grin. "Get some pain killers inside you. The being a hero part is done. You saved the girl, now go rest up and heal."

Javier rolled his eyes as he sank back against the cushions on his couch. "Fine, but text me when you hear anything or I'm coming back into work this afternoon."

Reid shook his head. "Nope, you're on leave, Jack's orders." Reid held up his hand as Javier went to protest. "But yes, you'll be kept up to date on everything and we'll see you back next Monday."

Addie walked him to the door. "Thanks, Reid."

"You're welcome. Call if you need anything at all. Callie will probably be over with the girls tomorrow, just because they're all nosey."

Adeline laughed at that knowing he adored Callie, who he called his sunshine, more than life. There was a time when she would've been envious of that but as she closed the door and turned back to find Javier watching her while Payton sat beside him with his iPad on her knee, she knew she'd found the very thing she didn't know she needed. A partner, a man who'd love her and her child, a man who made her heart race with one look.

"Do you need anything before I show Mia to her room?"

"No, I'm good here."

"Come on, monkey, let's go put your stuff away and show Mia which room will be hers."

Payton dropped the tablet and grasped her hand. Addie knew she'd never take the feel of her child's hand in hers for granted again. She'd almost lost her and if Juan had realised that Payton wasn't his, she would have. Never in her life had she been more grateful for friends like the ones she had now.

It made her think of Brand, Hustle, and Santa. Shadow, who'd literally melted into the night after the shootout at the Ravelino mansion, were apparently trying to locate them. The working theory was they were either so deep they had no access to comms or they were dead. She prayed they were alive but she honestly didn't know.

After a dinner of pie and chips smothered in mushy peas, which Payton had turned her nose up at and Mia had nibbled at, Addie took Payton up to give her a bath and put her to bed. Mia had insisted on clearing up and she'd sensed the woman needed the activity to keep busy.

"Tip your head back."

Payton did as she asked, giggling as the soapy water washed over her back. "Mommy, is Javier my daddy?"

Addie stilled, her heart beating fast as her throat went dry. She swallowed before continuing to rinse her daughter's curly blonde hair so much like Astrid's, who already adored her niece, and the feeling was very much mutual.

"No, sweetheart, he isn't."

"Is Mr Ravelino my daddy?"

Addie squeezed the water out of her child's hair and encouraged her to stand so she could wrap a towel around her. "No, that man isn't your father."

"Okay."

Addie thought she'd got away with it until Payton was just about asleep after she'd read her three stories about princesses and dragons that they'd picked up from the airport shop.

"Mommy?"

"Yes, my angel?"

"Will you tell me about him one day?"

A knot of pain pierced her heart, knowing she'd have to tell Payton what a selfish asshole her sperm donor was one day. "One day, sweetheart, yes."

She stayed listening to her child breathe peacefully and wondered what she dreamt of and if the ordeal of the last six months held any horror for her. She'd speak to Dr Sankey about a councillor for Payton and maybe even for herself. Savannah

Sankey had become more than the doctor who saved her since she'd woken from her coma, she'd become a friend to both her and Astrid.

Leaving the bedroom door open and the landing light on, she walked back downstairs and found Javier and Mia sitting in silence in the lounge. She stopped and looked between them, each lost in their own pain and fear and her heart ached for them. Could she be the bridge that brought them together again? Sitting beside Javier, she curled her feet under her legs and leaned on his good side, careful not to jar him in any way.

He'd at least agreed to some medication after dinner and his colour looked better for it. His hand landed on her thigh, warm and comforting and she forced her body not to react to his touch but failed. She doubted there'd ever be a time when she didn't react to his touch.

Blinking, she forced thoughts of Javier and how he made her body tingle away and focused on healing the rift between mother and son. "Mia, I want you to know how much it means to me that you cared for Payton when I couldn't. You'll never know how grateful I am."

Mia's face softened and the lines of stress around her mouth smoothed out making her look younger, allowing Addie to see the beauty of the woman who'd obviously suffered so much. Javier's hand tensed on her leg, and she laid her hand over his, urging him to relax. She felt the exhale go through him.

"I do know, sweet girl. A mother's love is hard to explain and I'm happy I was able to do that for you. I'm only sorry that I hurt my own son so much."

Javier stayed stoically silent beside her, and she nudged him gently. He glanced at her, and she could see the anguish he still carried over the mother he'd thought he'd lost.

"Tell me what happened, Mom. Explain to me how all of this came about."

Addie went to move, to give them some privacy and he stopped her. "No, you stay. I want you here." She sat down and cuddled into him, offering him whatever support he needed.

Mia looked between them for a beat before she began. "Your father wasn't a good man, Javier, but he also wasn't the monster you believe him to be. When we first met, he'd leave daisies on my doorstep each morning so that when I stepped outside, I had something pretty to look at. He used to say that he had me to think of and it was only fair I had the same beauty. We fell in love but as you know, my parents didn't want me to be with a poor man, no matter how much he loved me."

Javier lifted his hand and dropped it in defeat and confusion. "I know all this."

"Yes, you do but you were so young when he left, I don't think you ever really believed it."

"He left you, Mom, for a life of crime. You weren't enough for him. I wasn't enough."

"Oh, son, that's not true. He loved us. He still does. He left because we had no money, and he did one silly job and the cartel owned him. He left because he kept trying to refuse jobs and they came to the house. Juan Ravelino and his brother came to my house. They were only young men, but they threatened us and your father couldn't handle it. He left the very next day to go and be what they wanted him to be so we could live a life free from them."

Javier blinked in confusion his brow furrowed. "We lived in Mexico?"

"Yes, when you were very small. I fled after he left and came home to the US and did the best I could. Eventually, your father began making headlines and it pained me to see them, but I never stopped loving the man who left daisies for me."

"How did you end up disappearing?"

"I was at home one day when your father knocked on my door. He told me I had to leave and go into hiding. He was going to turn state's evidence against the cartel and there'd be blowback. He wanted us safe, but before he could get us out, they found us.

Ravelino took me as collateral to keep your father from talking about the cartel."

"Why did you never try to escape or try and reach out to me? I would've come for you."

Addie had tears running down her cheeks now and she sniffed when she heard the wobble in Javier's voice.

"Oh, Javi, I know you would have, but I agreed to stay without complaint if he left you alone and for some reason, Juan Ravelino agreed."

Addie felt a shudder go through Javier. "I thought you were dead. I grieved for you. I blamed him."

"I'm so sorry." Mia stood and crossed to her son and wrapped her arms around him as if he were still a boy, her eyes on her. A silent message passed between the two women who'd do anything for their children.

Mia pulled away and faced her son. "Can you forgive me?"

"Of course. I'm just glad you're back."

"Me too, son, and I want to be part of your life in any way you'll allow me."

Javier laughed. "Good because I have years' worth of laundry for you to put away."

Mia laughed and it was a beautiful sound and sight to see, and Addie felt blessed to be part of this reunion.

"Now, tell me how you two met."

Javier looked at her and winked, the joy on his face clear. They had a mountain of battles still to fight but for tonight, they had nothing but time.

"That's quite the story."

CHAPTER NINETEEN

"Mommy, Javi is teaching me Python."

Lopez glanced from the child sitting beside him on the couch to the woman who'd breathed life into his world. Addie was wiping flour from her hands on a dishtowel and smiling at them. His pulse pounded in his neck as he looked at her, his body always hyper-aware of her, the need to demolish the distance between them making his legs tingle.

"Oh yeah and why is that?"

Addie must have sensed how he felt because she moved to sit on the edge of the couch next to him, her breast brushing against his shoulder, her heat and scent making his senses swim with a heady feeling of love and desire. The light touch on his arm had him looking up at her radiant gaze.

She was so fucking beautiful it was hard to look at her sometimes —or any time really—and not give in to the need to touch her skin or kiss her full lips. Her brow quirked and he grinned, unrepentant of his desire for her.

"I'm going to be a super spy and superspies need to be able to get in places and Javi is going to teach me."

Lopez swallowed his laughter, not wanting Payton to think he was laughing at her. The last six weeks had been the best of his life. The physical therapy with Waggs was hell but he was fully healed now and back to full strength. His mother and Addie were as thick as thieves and having her back in his life was a gift he'd never take for granted.

The revelations about his father had been slow to process and he wasn't sure if he'd ever equate the man he knew as a contract killer with the man his mother described. She went by Mia now, apparently it had been what his dad called her, and Payton knew her as Aunt Mia, so she stuck with it.

"Hey, pipsqueak, I didn't say I'd help you break the law."

He tugged on one of Payton's pigtails and she gave him a cheeky grin which made his heart tighten with love for her. In the space of a few weeks she'd made a space for herself in his heart, along with her mother and now he couldn't imagine his life without either of them and he hoped he never had to.

"Payton, come help me taste test these cookies," his mother called from the kitchen, and he laughed as she abandoned her life of crime for cookies.

Hooking his arm around Addie's waist he pulled her onto his lap, his hand finding the warm skin of her back under her shirt. Addie looped her arms around his neck and leaned into him for a kiss.

It was slow and leisurely as if they had all the time in the world, which he hoped they did. It didn't stop him from taking over, cupping her head with his free hand, and deepening the kiss until she was breathing hard, her hands moving over his chest.

"We can't, not here," she murmured against his lips.

"I want you in my bed tonight." He knew she understood his meaning because she rested her head against his and nodded.

"Okay. We should explain to her so she's not confused."

Addie had been firm that she didn't want Payton to be put through any more stress and sharing her mother with a man for the first time in her life was a lot after everything else she'd been through. He'd agreed, so the last six weeks had been stolen moments with her heading back to her own bed before Payton woke up.

It had been easier after his mother found her own place two weeks ago at her own initiation. She'd moved into a two-bedroom flat in the same building as Reid and Callie lived in by the river and she loved it.

"Want me to help you explain it?"

"Yes, please. You want this parenting thing then we do the hard bits together too."

Her smile lit him up with pride and love. He did want all of it, every second of it with her. "I want it all, Addie. I never knew I could love anyone like I love you. I never believed in soulmates until I saw Alex and Evelyn and then Blake and Pax. Even as I watched my friends find the one person who completed them, I never believed it would happen to me. Not until I met you. I'm better for loving you and each day I wake up excited for the day because I know it includes you."

"Javier." Her face softened; her eyes glistened with love for him.

"It's true, I love you so damn much and I love that little girl too. I couldn't love her more if she carried my DNA."

"Do you love Aunt Mia too?"

Lopez and Addie glanced to the door to see Payton watching them with her head cocked to the side. He held out his arm to her and she ran to them and jumped up on his lap with her mother. He held them both tight in his arms as his mother watched from the doorway, a soft look of love on her face.

"Yes, Payton, I love Aunt Mia too. She's my mom and I love her a lot. I love you but differently. I love your mom as well, and that's different again."

"Kinda like how I love Mom 'cos she bakes for me and reads me bedtime stories and does stuff for me, like makes me hot chocolate with sprinkles, but I love you 'cos you play on computers and have a cool job?"

His heart was almost full to bursting with her words. "Yes, something like that."

"Okay, cool. Can I have my own room?"

He wanted to praise the gods as she gave them the perfect opener and he saw his mother smirk as she walked back into the kitchen.

"Yes. How about your mom shares with me and we can decorate your room how you like it?"

"What about Mommy? Can't she decorate too?"

"She can do whatever she likes."

"Okay. I want black and purple."

Addie laughed. "I don't think so, munchkin, but let's talk more after dinner."

Lopez let Addie go knowing tonight he'd get to have her all to himself for the entire night. Kids made a person nothing if not inventive. He picked up the phone and dialled Alex. They'd been invited to a barbecue at Alex and Evelyn's to celebrate Elena's birth.

"Lopez, what can I do for you?"

"Hey, Alex. I just wanted to know if you needed us to bring anything tomorrow?"

"Nah, Evelyn's parents are here. Her mother is cooking up a storm and I just got kicked out of my own kitchen."

"Ouch. That must have stung."

"I know, right, but it gives me more time with Elena."

It was a fool who couldn't hear the pride and love in Alex's voice when he spoke of his daughter. "Enjoy it."

"I am. Never thought I'd have this so I'm cherishing every second. Hey, you hear Valentina is being seconded by Jack to work with Shadow for the foreseeable future?"

"Yeah, how does Rafe feel about that? I thought he and his sister worked well together."

"Yeah, they do but Shadow needed someone with her skills."

"Makes sense then. Speaking of Shadow, do they have any leads on Hansen?"

"Nope, he's a ghost."

"Fuck. I just wish we knew for certain he'd leave Addie alone."

"Yeah, I get that. It can't be nice knowing he's out there. But at least the US has agreed that Adeline and Astrid aren't persons of interest and they won't ever come after them."

"True, there is that. Of course, having the Monarch on your friend's list isn't a bad place to be."

"Amen, but neither is it fun having her as an enemy, as Evelyn and I can attest to."

"I guess for now we take the wins and keep our guards up."

"Yup. Right, I'm going to let you go and I'll see you tomorrow. You're bringing Mia, right?"

"Yes, of course."

"Cool, catch ya later."

Lopez hung up hating that Hansen was still out there and free after everything he'd done. He wanted him locked away for the rest of his miserable life. He may have let Shadow take this case but neither he nor Jack had let it go. That man had hurt the women they loved and that would never be allowed to fly.

Later that night as he lay in bed with his arms around Addie, her back to his front, her body satiated from the two orgasms he'd given her and the one spectacular one he'd had, he tried to remember what it felt like without her in his life and couldn't. He wondered again how he'd ever lived without her and realised he probably hadn't been, at least not to the fullest.

"I can hear your brain ticking."

Lopez squeezed her tighter and kissed her bare shoulder, the skin warm and silky beneath his lips. "Sorry."

She turned in the darkness to look at him. "What's wrong?" She could see through him as if he was glass.

"Just thinking how lucky I am to have you and how much I love you."

Addie rolled in his arms and snuggled closer to his body. The weather was going through a cooler patch as the end of summer began. Her fingers spread over the healed bullet wound on his shoulder. "I love you so much. If I had to go through everything again to get me here with you, I would. Not the bit where Payton was taken but the rest was worth it as it led me here."

Lopez rolled so he was lying between her thighs, his chest brushing her hard nipples, his arms braced either side of her head. "Yeah?"

"Yeah."

He dipped his head and kissed her, letting her feel every bit of the love he felt for her. Her hands roamed his back and ass as he eased his cock into her tight heat, a groan of pleasure slipping from his lips. He made love to her slowly, building their pleasure, coaxing her climax from her with stolen kisses and whispered words.

"You're so perfect, Addie."

"I'm close, Javier."

"Let go, beautiful, I'm right behind you."

His thumb circled her clit and a few strokes later she shattered, crying his name as he kissed her and shuddered his own climax into her body.

This right here was perfection.

CHAPTER TWENTY

LOPEZ WOKE WITH A START, his body going rigid, his heart banging in his chest the following night and he stilled, listening for the sound that had woken him. It was still dark out and as he looked at the clock, he realised it was two am and he'd only been asleep an hour. He glanced at Addie and debated letting her sleep. They'd spent the day with Alex and Evelyn and all their friends celebrating and it had been perfect. Addie had let her hair down and he'd spent most of his time either watching her laugh or laughing with her.

She'd been tired when they got back though and had fallen asleep almost immediately after her head hit the pillow. With a split-second decision he decided to leave her sleeping and check it out. Grabbing his sidearm and checking his watch was active, he slid silently out of bed and walked to the bedroom door.

He checked the app on his watch. It didn't show any breaches in security on the house and his property was still on the highest alert with Hansen still on the run. The CIA had maintained he was undercover and couldn't be reached when they'd spoken to the director, but they all knew that was bullshit.

Poking his head into Payton's room he saw she was fast asleep and spread-eagled across the double bed, the pale pink quilt cover hanging off the edge, and her unicorn teddy still clasped in her hand. The sight made him smile despite feeling that something was off. He moved to the top of the stairs and heard the sound that must have woken him again. A light tapping sound that he couldn't place.

Weapon up, he crept down the stairs and the sound grew louder. He immediately spotted the small open window in the living room and swept his gaze around the room. It would have been impossible for anyone to get in through there but then it also should've triggered the alarms. He knew for damn sure he hadn't left that window open, and he checked the house each night like a fucking guard to ensure his family were safe.

Noting the house was secure and nobody was inside, he hit the alert on his watch to let the team know there'd been a break in security. He was about to go back upstairs and wake Addie when he saw him on the back lawn. Joel Hansen was standing in the middle of his backyard, hands by his sides as if he were waiting for him.

Lopez turned and walked to the backdoor. He hit the security lights and nothing happened. Figured Hansen would take those out first. The man might be a complete asshole, but he was still a highly trained one. Lopez again debated heading upstairs to wake Addie but if he did that, he might lose his chance to get his hands on Hansen and he very much wanted that.

He opened the door, and the man didn't flinch, his hands by his sides in some sort of submissive gesture that didn't ring true. What was his game here? Lopez knew that backup was only five minutes out at best.

"Hands in the air, Hansen!" Lopez moved forward slowly, his bare feet cold on the wet grass.

Hansen raised his hands. "I want to see Adeline."

Lopez fought the snarl when he said her name. "No fucking way. You don't get the chance to try and weasel your way out of what you did. You speak to me."

"I know what you think of me."

Lopez could almost taste the fury that was so intense his body almost shook with it. "You have no fucking clue what I think."

"I know you hate me, that you think I used her and Astrid."

"You fucking did use them, you piece of shit, and I'm going to make sure you pay for every single life you ruined."

Hansen glanced up at the same time Lopez felt her behind him. Her hand on his back anchored him from losing his mind and shooting Hansen dead right then, but he wasn't his father, and he couldn't kill an unarmed man.

"What the hell do you want?" Addie stepped beside him, and he hated that Hansen was seeing her in short pyjamas, still sleep tousled and beautiful.

"I just want to talk."

"So, talk."

"Is she mine?"

Lopez swallowed, a muscle jumping in his clenched jaw as he tried to contain his anger. He wanted to answer for her but knew he couldn't.

"She's mine and nothing to do with you."

Hansen moved to step forward and Lopez snarled. "Stay the fuck there. I'm just looking for an excuse to put a bullet in your head, so give me one."

Hansen froze and glanced at Addie as if looking for support.

"You heard him."

"Am I Payton's biological father?"

Adeline shook her head. "You know the answer to that, you piece of shit. Yet you still handed her over to Juan for cold, hard cash."

Lopez moved his body closer to Addie to try and soothe her fury, not because he wanted her to go easy on the man in front of her but because he hated her upset.

"Go check on Payton, Addie. We don't want her waking and walking into this shit storm."

Addie nodded and glanced at Hansen with a lip curl.

"On your knees, Hansen."

CONSIDER THIS AN OLIVE BRANCH. *I'll leave you alone as long as you leave me alone. Look for me and I'll take away everything you love.*

"FUCKING PIECE OF SHIT BASTARD." Lopez sucked in air through his nose to try and keep calm and stop himself from punching something.

"Shadow will handle it. Let him think we're walking away." Jack looked around the area. "My bet is he's watching so make a show of accepting his terms."

"Are you fucking kidding me, Jack?" Lopez bellowed not having to fake the anger he was feeling for this performance.

"I said fucking stand down, Lopez. We have bigger fish to fry than Hansen. Let the CIA handle him."

"You really want me to let this go?"

"Yes, for Payton's sake let it go and move on. You have everything you need here, let Hansen walk."

He raised his voice so that anyone watching would hear him clearly. "This isn't like you, Jack."

"I have bigger fish to fry than some failed spook."

"I want it on record I'm against this. I'll do it but only for Addie and Payton."

"Good, now get yourself over to my place so my woman can make sure her sister and niece are safe. She made up the spare room. We'll finish up here. It's over for us for now."

The last was said quietly just for him to hear. Lopez nodded and walked to the car where Addie was cradling a still sleeping Payton in the back seat.

He climbed in beside her and wrapped her in his arms, kissing her head and thanking God she was safe.

"Everything okay?"

"Yeah, we're safe. Hansen won't be back."

He believed that to be true. Hansen had bigger fish to fry. Eidolon would walk away but Shadow wouldn't.

EPILOGUE

ADELINE FIXED the final bobby pin into Astrid's hair and stepped back to survey her sister in the mirror. "You look absolutely stunning. Every inch the princess."

Astrid's laugh was warm, her smile radiant as she met her eyes in the glass. "I should in this get-up. I can't believe the Queen loaned me one of her tiaras." Astrid touched the diamond tiara that had once been worn by Queen Victoria with reverence.

"It is pretty surreal. But then I never thought I'd get to see my baby sister walk down the aisle, let alone be her maid of honour."

Astrid stood, the layers of her fairy-tale beaded tulle and satin ball gown falling around her legs, the layered handkerchief skirt swishing softly. She gripped her hands, just the two of them sharing these final few moments alone before she became Mrs Jack Granger. Her eyes teared and she blinked rapidly.

"Oh God, stop, or I'll cry too and then Mustique will be in here kicking my ass for ruining her make-up job."

Adeline laughed. The women of Zenobi were fierce but if they loved you, they'd die for you. They'd saved Astrid when she couldn't, and she'd never forget that. "I just want you to know how happy I am for you, bumble. I couldn't have chosen a better man for you than Jack. He looks at you like you're the air he needs to breathe, and you deserve that."

"I never thought I could love someone like I do him. I can't explain how he makes me feel, I just know that I'll love him until the day I die."

Adeline shook her head. "You don't have to, I know."

Astrid cocked her head. "Lopez is a good man, and he loves you like Jack loves me."

"I know. I'm so lucky. Sometimes it feels like a dream and the way he loves Payton you'd never believe he wasn't her real father. You know she started calling him Daddy when we're at home now."

"No. Oh, bee, that's so sweet. Can you believe Mom and Dad actually travelled for the wedding? I was convinced Mom would pass out when I said the Queen would be here for the ceremony."

"Are you surprised? It's the freaking Queen, Astrid. This might be the norm for you now but the rest of us are still trying to catch up."

Astrid giggled as a knock came on the door.

"Astrid it's time," their father called through the door.

The reunion and revelations had been a lot for her parents. Finding out the child they'd thought dead was alive and they had a grandchild was a shock, but they'd been so happy and there'd been a lot of tears. Javier had been by her side through it all, never wavering or pushing her, just standing beside her.

The last four months had been the best of her life and she was excited to see what the future held for them all. Pax had given birth to a daughter and the Eidolon family was growing with Princess Taamira and Liam announcing they were expecting a baby next spring.

Adeline kept a step behind her sister, holding Payton's hand as she walked down the aisle. Her eyes scanned the crowd noting how handsome Jack, Will his best man, his friend Zack, as well as Alex and Decker looked in their morning suits. Their ties matched the soft, dusky mauve of the bridesmaid's dress she wore.

When her eyes landed on the man she loved, her heart lit up with love for him as he smiled back at her. He looked gorgeous in a dark grey suit and a tie to match her dress, with a cream rose in his buttonhole.

Adeline gave him a soft smile as he stood beside Mia who'd been the biggest blessing. She adored Payton and was a wonderful friend to her, almost a surrogate mother in some ways. She loved her own mother, but Mia knew her story, even the bits she didn't want her to and she understood that sometimes fear won. When that happened, she stepped up and gave her and Javier the time they needed to get back on track.

The ceremony was beautiful, with Jack and Astrid saying their own vows and there wasn't a dry eye in the house after that, even the big, bad men of Eidolon seemed affected, casting loving looks to the women they stood beside. She couldn't resist looking at Javier and he mouthed the words I love you making her blink hard to stop the tears. She blew him a kiss which he pretended to catch, and she loved how he didn't care who saw him being mushy or that he could be that way with her. In every other way, he was an alpha male.

He never let her car run out of fuel, he always made sure he was the one to lock the house up at night and make sure they were safe. He never let her pay for anything, insisting she keep her money for herself and yet he didn't treat her like her opinion didn't matter. He always wanted her opinion and would gladly defer to her with certain things. They worked, that was the truth as simple as it was.

As they exited into the large courtyard of Eastnor Castle, she saw Jack and Astrid talking to the Queen and the Duke before they left to head home. They'd wanted to come, the relationship between the two families dating back years and years but hadn't wanted to steal the limelight from the happy couple.

"Hey, you, can I ensure a slot on your dance card later?"

Adeline looked up with a smile at the familiar, deep voice and into the eyes of the man she loved. "You sure can, handsome, but don't tell my boyfriend or he might get jealous."

She saw his eyes flare and darken. He growled before he captured her mouth in a deep soulful kiss that left her heart racing. "Tell him your dance card is fully booked indefinitely."

Adeline gripped his biceps through the shirt and felt the power in his body and her own went liquid with desire. "Oh yeah?"

"Yeah."

Her body flushed and she wanted his hands on her despite only feeling them a few hours ago. She was insatiable with this man, and he felt the same. It was as though they had a hunger that instead of being satiated, got worse with every moment they spent together.

"You look beautiful, Addie."

"You told me that already."

"It was worth repeating."

"You look delicious."

"Am I a cream puff?"

Addie threw back her head and laughed. "You're definitely not a cream puff. More of a juicy steak."

"This conversation is ridiculous, but I love you anyway."

"I love you, too." She glanced around her gaze looking for Payton. "Where's Payton?" Her heart always stuttered a little when she couldn't find her for a split second, but it was getting better.

Javier turned angling his body towards Waggs and Willow. "With AJ and Maggie."

"Oh, good."

"Addie, you're needed for photos!" Pax called, waving her over, as Blake stood beside her holding his baby daughter in his arms.

"Duty calls but save me a dance."

She dropped a kiss on his lips and rushed off toward the happy couple. For the rest of the day every time Addie got a second to go find her man, someone wanted to chat, or Astrid needed something. She missed him even though they were in the same room, and he kept making eye contact with her. She'd been on the top table with the other members of the wedding party and Javier had sat with Payton and Mia at a table with Waggs, Willow, AJ, Gunner, and Lacey.

She was about to head to him when Astrid announced it was time to toss the wedding bouquet.

"Okay, all you single ladies get your butts lined up here." Astrid came over and started lining them all up, shoving her between Bebe and Laverne at the front. "Okay, are you all ready?"

Astrid faced away from them all and Addie grinned at her sister as she began to swing her hand to toss the flowers over her head. Then she stopped, turned, and walked toward her and handed her the bouquet. Addie looked at her in confusion.

"I love you, Addie."

Then she gave her a slight nudge and Addie turned to see Javier on one knee holding a ring box out to her. Tears of shock and joy blurred her eyes and she put her hand over her mouth in surprise. He looked nervous but so handsome and her heart burst with love for him.

"Adeline, since the second I laid eyes on you, I felt like I'd found the missing piece of me. You make me a better man every day, and I wake up knowing that whatever I face will work out because I have you by my side. I promise to love you until the day I die and even beyond. Please make me the happiest man alive and say you'll marry me?"

A sob tore through her throat at his declaration and question that followed. "Yes, yes I'll marry you." Through the broken sobs he heard her and the next second she was in his arms, and everyone was cheering as he kissed her as if there was nobody else in the room, just the two of them in a blissful bubble.

He pulled away and pulled the diamond teardrop-shaped ring from the box and slid it on her finger. "I love you, so much."

"I love you. I can't believe you did all this. Did everyone know?"

Javier held her close, his warm hands on her waist, her hands resting on his chest. "Payton knew about an hour ago which is why I had to keep her away from you. I wasn't sure if she could keep the secret, but I had to ask her first. Your Mom, Dad, Astrid, and Jack knew. It was actually her idea to do it here."

Adeline looked to Astrid who was standing with Jack. He had Payton in his arms and she was giggling at them as her sister and new brother-in-law raised their glasses of champagne to her.

"Best. Day. Ever."

"Yeah, it is, and you can tell that boyfriend of yours that your future husband said to get lost."

His words were filled with laughter, but she was serious. "When I'm with you, Javier, nobody else exists for me."

He kissed her, his lips firm and the room cheered again and then she was swamped by people congratulating them and offering hugs and kisses. It was later while she was catching her breath beside her sister and chatting with Savannah Sankey that she got the chance to thank her sister for sharing the limelight with her on her special day.

"Nobody I'd rather share it with, bee."

Then the room went dark, and the spotlights came on, and an even bigger shocker happened, but this one she knew all about and had helped arrange. All of the Eidolon men including her now fiancé were lined up on the dance floor. Bruno Mars, Uptown Funk began to play and as they'd rehearsed a hundred times, the men began to dance.

Astrid was shocked at first but quickly got into it, whooping and hollering and she had to admit it was the sexiest thing she'd ever seen. All those hot men dancing in their suits, normally so serious because of what they did, were all enjoying themselves. Even Decker, the lone single wolf in the pack now, seemed to be enjoying himself. She wondered if his time was coming and hoped it was. He deserved a woman who'd make him smile after everything he'd been through.

As the song ended, Javier made a beeline for her, and she wound her arms around him.

"Ready to give me that dance, gorgeous?"

"Oh yeah, handsome, show me your moves."

DECKER SNEAK PEEK

Savannah smiled to herself as she watched Astrid and Jack dance surrounded by their friends and family, especially Adeline and Lopez, who after a very rough start had found love. It filled her bruised heart with hope that maybe one day she'd find that same kind of love. Not the fake façade her ex-husband had offered her before deciding monogamy wasn't for him and forgetting to let her know.

Leaning against the wall of the beautiful castle a sigh escaped her as she sipped on her champagne. It had been a day of surprises, especially as the actual Queen had attended the ceremony, and her now friend and former patient, Adeline, getting a surprise proposal followed by a dance from Jack and his friends that had finished off a wonderful day.

She felt him before she saw him. Something about the cool, clever, handsome profiler who seemed to dislike her immensely rattled her. Perhaps because it was unusual for someone to dislike her so much when she'd done nothing wrong to them that she was aware of, or maybe it was because she found him so damned attractive that her heart sped up at the sight of him, despite the unnecessary barbs he threw her way.

Savannah refused to turn and acknowledge his presence. She was there first and if he wanted to disturb her peace then he could make the first move at conversation.

"I suppose you buy into all this happily ever after nonsense too?"

Savannah hid the smile at her tiny victory and turned, her eyebrow raised in question. "Nonsense?"

"That mystical happy ever after."

Savannah ran a critical eye over Mark Decker, who looked as delectably unattainable as ever in his three-piece grey suit that fit like it was made for him, which it most likely was. He was beyond handsome, tall, his dark hair swept back from his forehead, and if she guessed correctly, it had a slight wave in it. Deep brown eyes that seemed to hold a wealth of secrets, long, inky black lashes and high cheekbones which complimented a jaw cut from marble, which was probably cut from the same template that had been used on Michelangelo's David.

Savannah had no idea why he was so damn off with her when he was perfectly delightful with everyone else. Especially when his eyes swept over her from head to toe, a hot look of desire in them. It gave her a giddy feeling to be wanted by him when it was clear he didn't want to want her.

Turning away and back to the scene on the dance floor, she cocked her head at his question. Watching the love before her it was hard to understand how he could think that way.

Looking up at him again she was struck by how tall he was. She was five feet seven so by no means short, but he towered over her, his shoulders wide and powerful. She knew he was built, had seen him after a training session in the gym at his work and still had fantasies about it.

He continued to watch the floor not looking at her.

"I think the people in front of us are proof it's real, Mark."

She saw his jaw flex and wondered what she'd said this time to upset him.

"It never lasts, that's the problem with perfection."

"I don't think any of them would say it's perfect, but it's perfect for them and that's what counts. Have you never been in love, Mark?" She didn't know what made her ask the question, whether it was the champagne or the atmosphere, but he almost winced at her words, and she knew she'd hit a tender spot.

"Once."

He said no more, and she regretted asking knowing she'd caused him pain and that had never been her plan. She was a healer at heart, always had been, and still was, her goal always to help not harm.

"Tell me, Dr Sankey, do you get a kick out of poking your nose in where it's not wanted?"

Savannah sucked in a breath at the hurtful comment she knew was said for that very reason. Mark Decker was acting like a wounded bear and lashing out. As much as she wanted to be the bigger person, she wouldn't be an emotional punching bag for him or anyone else. "I think this little discussion, if you can call it that, is over. If you'll excuse me, I need some air." Without waiting for his reply, she pulled her wrap tighter around her shoulders and walked onto the balcony behind her, leaving Mark Decker to his own misery.

The night was clear, the sky obsidian with millions of stars twinkling above her. Savannah sucked in a breath of the cool, fresh air and let it out slowly. She loved nights like this when it felt like the sky was the limit and endless possibilities were laid out. Seeing the love surrounding her today reminded her of her own solitary existence.

She'd put everything into her mission to become the best neurosurgeon she could be, and had made so many sacrifices, none of which she regretted. Her marriage had been a sham from the very beginning. Andy Farr was one of the top neurosurgeons in the country, he was also arrogant, conceited, and in the beginning, charming. She'd mistaken his late nights and missed dinners as a commitment to his job. God knew she was the same but while she was working, he was screwing around.

She gave a shake of her head, banishing thoughts of the man who'd broken her heart. He didn't deserve the space in her head she was giving him. It was almost two years now and their divorce had been finalised the previous week. Andy had been hell-bent on winning her back, blocking the divorce at every turn until he'd gotten one of the scrub nurses pregnant and she'd forced his hand. Savannah actually felt sorry for her. Andy would never stay faithful, and she knew now what she'd thought was love was more hero worship. For all his faults, and there were many, he was a wonderful surgeon.

Savannah felt movement behind her and knew who it was without turning around. His cologne was distinctive to him, and she hated the fact she could pick it out after he'd been such a jerk to her before. She turned to leave, not wanting another sparring session with Mark Decker, and avoided eye contact.

"Don't go." A firm hand landed on her forearm, stopping her momentum and she glanced up at him. He really was sinfully handsome yet so distant and guarded. "Please. I'm sorry I was rude to you earlier."

Her lips twitched with a smile, knowing that the apology must have cost him. He didn't strike her as a man who easily admitted when he was wrong. No, Mark Decker was a man with exacting standards for himself and those around him. Savannah resumed her place, looking out over the beautifully lit gardens of the Castle with the stars above and the backdrop of laughter and music coming from behind them.

Savannah sipped her champagne and angled slightly towards Mark. He was looking out over the landscape, and it gave her a moment to study the sexy yet unreadable man, to wonder what made him the person he was, what secrets he held. He looked so proud and strong, like a warrior of old and she knew he must have scars inside to have earned the pain she saw deep within him. His dark hair was combed perfectly, and she had the urge to run her fingers through it and mess him up a bit, just to see his reaction. The image of him sweaty and unguarded the one time she'd seen him with his friends popped into her thoughts, and she wondered what kind of woman would be able to make a man like him love her and what had happened to make him so cold. "Why don't you like me?"

Mark angled his body to her, one perfectly arched brow raised in question. "I don't dislike you. I hardly know you."

"No, you don't, yet I still get the feeling I've done something to annoy you and I don't know what it is."

"You haven't done anything to *annoy me* as you put it, Dr Sankey."

Savannah snorted and rolled her eyes. "If you say so."

"What does that mean?"

Savannah seemed to have his full attention as he turned more towards her. "You're snide, cold, and rude. You argued with every assessment I made on Adeline even though I'm a leading expert in my field, and you've made it more than clear that you can't stand being around me."

"Seems like you've given this a lot of thought."

Savannah shrugged. "People generally like me, so when someone doesn't, it bugs me."

Mark stepped closer his eyes travelling over her face in a slow perusal which had her breath hitching and her body tingling. He lifted one hand from his pocket and curled a finger around a strand of her long hair, which she'd left down to hang in waves over her shoulders for once.

"You have this all wrong, Dr Sankey. I do like you." He frowned as he twirled her hair between strong tanned fingers. "You have the prettiest eyes."

His compliment caught her off guard and she gasped. Decker dipped his head slowly and she closed her eyes waiting for his kiss, her heart pounding in her chest. She'd never wanted a kiss more than she did this one.

His lips brushed hers gently, almost a whisper and then it was like fire raged through her and she gripped the lapels of his jacket, wanting him closer as his lips, firm and sure, drugged her. Her sigh allowed him to move his tongue along her bottom lip, his hands on her hips now pulling her closer to his heated body.

It was everything a first kiss should be, confident, powerful, and mind-blowing. Her body was alight with desire for him, her hands wanting to feel his skin beneath her fingers. To see if he was as warm as she imagined and if his body was as hard as the glimpses of muscle had hinted at.

"Deck! Oh, shit. Sorry."

Decker pulled abruptly away as if she'd scalded him and looked at her with shock and distaste, putting distance between them as he turned to Waggs, who was looking sheepish as he stood at the door to the balcony.

"What can I do for you, Waggs?"

Was she imagining it or was his voice deeper and more gravely than before? It was hard to tell with his stiff back to her.

"Sorry to interrupt, but Jack wants a quick word."

Humiliation slammed through Savannah as he ignored her as if what they'd shared meant nothing, worse, was a mistake.

"No interruption. I was just placating Dr Sankey's delicate ego."

Savannah felt molten heat move through her veins, this time fury and anger replacing the embarrassment from seconds before. "You bastard."

Savannah pulled the shawl tighter around her shoulders and moved through the balcony door with her head held high as she nodded at Waggs who looked unhappy. She made it inside and slouched against the frame to catch her breath and calm her anger. Hot tears of shame over falling for his charm and sexual manipulation burned her eyes.

"Fucking hell, Deck, that was a dick thing to do."

She could hear Waggs speaking through the door but didn't stop to listen. She had no interest in what Mark Decker had to say. She was done with men who didn't respect her or value her. It was time to go home to her gorgeous three bedroom detached house and snuggle in her bed with a good book.

Savannah took a taxi home. She'd had too much to drink to drive and having seen the devastation alcohol and driving could have on the brain, she never took the chance. As she paid the driver and stepped out of the cab, the nude heels that were much higher than the usual crocs she wore for work, pinched. They looked great, and her legs looked a mile long in them and they gave her ass some sway, but she'd be so glad to kick them off. As she neared the door, her steps faltered. Across her front door in bright red paint was the word murderer. It seemed like her day wouldn't be getting any better from this point on.

WANT A FREE SHORT STORY?

Sign up for Maddie's Newsletter using the link below and receive a free copy of the short story, Fortis: Where it all Began.

When hard-nosed SAS operator, Zack Cunningham is forced to work a mission with the fiery daughter of the American General, sparks fly. As those heated looks turn into scorching hot stolen kisses, a forbidden love affair begins that neither had expected.

Just as life is looking perfect disaster strikes and Ava Drake is left wondering if she will ever see the man she loves again.

https://dl.bookfunnel.com/cyrjtv3tta

BOOKS BY MADDIE WADE

Fortis Security

Healing Danger (Dane and Lauren)

Stolen Dreams (Nate and Skye)

Love Divided (Jace and Lucy)

Secret Redemption (Zack and Ava)

Broken Butterfly (Zin and Celeste)

Arctic Fire (Kanan and Roz)

Phoenix Rising (Daniel and Megan)

Nate & Skye Wedding Novella

Digital Desire (Will and Aubrey)

Paradise Ties: A Fortis Wedding Novella (Jace and Lucy & Dane and Lauren)

Wounded Hearts (Drew and Mara)

Scarred Sunrise (Smithy and Lizzie)

Zin and Celeste: A Fortis Family Christmas

Fortis Boxset 1 (Books 1-3)

Fortis Boxset 2 (Books 4-7.5

Eidolon

Alex

Blake

Reid

Liam

Mitch

Gunner

Waggs

Jack

Lopez

Decker

———

Alliance Agency Series (co-written with India Kells)
Deadly Alliance

Knight Watch

Hidden Obsession

Lethal Justice

Innocent Target

Power Play

———

Ryoshi Delta (part of Susan Stoker's Police and Fire: Operation Alpha World)
Condor's Vow

Sandstorm's Promise

Hawk's Honor

Omega's Oath

———

Tightrope Duet

Tightrope One

Tightrope Two

———

Angels of the Triad

01 Sariel

———

Other Worlds

Keeping Her Secrets *Suspenseful Seduction World* (Samantha A. Cole's World)

Finding English *Police and Fire: Operation Alpha* (Susan Stoker's world)

ABOUT THE AUTHOR

Contact Me

If stalking an author is your thing and I sure hope it is then here are the links to my social media pages.

If you prefer your stalking to be more intimate, then my group Maddie's Minxes will welcome you with open arms.

General Email: info.maddiewade@gmail.com
Email: maddie@maddiewadeauthor.co.uk
Website: http://www.maddiewadeauthor.co.uk
Facebook page: https://www.facebook.com/maddieuk/
Facebook group: https://www.facebook.com/groups/546325035557882/
Amazon Author page: amazon.com/author/maddiewade
Goodreads: https://www.goodreads.com/author/show/14854265.Maddie_Wade
Bookbub: https://partners.bookbub.com/authors/3711690/edit
Twitter: @mwadeauthor
Pinterest: @maddie_wade
Instagram: Maddie Author

Printed in Great Britain
by Amazon

23522110R00108